SILKS

A Catherine Kint Mystery

HUGH MCGINLAY

Story by

Hugh McGinlay
&
Adam Palmer

First published by Clan Destine Press in 2023

Clan Destine Press
PO Box 121, Bittern
Victoria, 3918 Australia

National Library of Australia Cataloguing-In-Publication data:

McGinlay, Hugh

SILKS

ISBN: 978-1-922904-43-0 (paperback)

ISBN: 978-1-922904-44-7 (eBook)

Cover Design by © Willsin Rowe
Design & Typesetting by Clan Destine Press

www.clandestinepress.net

This one is for Eliza,
a person so eccentric that she ran off and *left* the circus.

1

People curse the cold, but it can be a wonderful aphrodisiac.
~Nealamber Singh

Some Melbourne winter nights, the city itself screams: don't go out. The wind howls: I am the furious wrath of the south. I will hurt you. I will wither your attempts to smile through it. There is no good time here. No rock and roll will keep you warm. You're done. Stay home. Cower. Show me you are afraid.

It screams: the nerve of people, to build a city this close to Antarctica.

Some nights, the scream is a furious billowing wind that cuts through skin. Other nights, it's an ancient, cold, strident note that leaches warmth and hope, barking ice into the bones of anyone foolish enough to ignore it, or unfortunate enough to have no choice. Worst of it is, it goes forever. Time changes to some Narnian curse every June in the capital of Victoria. Ask anyone who's endured it.

Some nights, going out in Melbourne is akin to fighting a war in Russia, and you can ask two of the most famous short men in history how that worked out.

Catherine Kint – who was incidentally taller than Napoleon but shorter than Adolf, and considerably less driven to war – believed in ignoring weather unless it behaved. On a night like this, it proved difficult, but it was necessary. She'd been caught in a shower as she left her apartment and icy stabs of water still trickled from her bob onto her neck, thirty-five minutes after she'd left Brunswick for Footscray. Her Vespa wasn't much shelter against the cold or the rain.

She shivered as she crossed the threshold into the Footscray community hall, instantly feeling as if her cheeks were thawing as the heaters worked their magic.

Catherine made her money through making hats, including the one she could see across the room. The fact that so many of her clients gifted her with free tickets to things was a wonderful fringe benefit. A sweetener in a life spent making beautiful things and talking to interesting people and having the occasional car chase.

Across the room, crowded with faces and, just above them, purple tinsel everywhere, she caught Boris' eye. He smiled enthusiastically but without showing teeth as he negotiated the crowd between them, holding glasses of sparkling white wine in both hands high above his bearded face. Within a minute, Catherine had taken a spot away from the door and Boris had found her.

Boris eased his bulk between two groups of women and walked the last step to her. 'I knew you wouldn't be far away so I got two glasses.'

Catherine took one and held out her hand for the other, eyebrow raised. 'You should have got one for yourself, dear.'

Boris deflated only a little. 'One at a time for you tonight. You know the price they're charging for these?'

'With a man like you in my life, I thought I didn't have to. Plus,' she toasted the room, 'there can be no greater cause to drink for than the circus, no?'

Boris took a large sip of his sparkling. 'Personally, I can think of true love and ending world poverty.'

Catherine sighed. 'Yes, which will still be around to drink to tomorrow. The circus is a reflection of the world it performs for and reminds us to retain our sense of wonder.'

A troupe of performers swarmed the lobby in a pre-show surprise preview. Six women, in purple and black tights and leotards, pushed back the crowd to give them a three metre circle and proceeded to make a human pyramid as easily as Boris would have fallen off one. They almost looked like one entity as they performed.

An acrobat with flaming dyed red hair broke off laterally, danced around the formation before joining it to become the apex. Once atop the structure, the acrobat smiled carnivorously at the audience before back flipping to the floor, landing nimbly. The audience clapped appreciatively as the tumblers disappeared backstage.

'Which one is your friend?'

'None of them. The manager is a client and almost a friend. A marvellous woman called Virginia. Look for the best hat here and you'll find her.'

Boris scanned the crowded room. It was as full of vibrancy as the outside was empty of warmth. 'Virginia, huh?'

'Don't get any ideas, sir. I'm pretty sure she'd be more interested in yours truly.'

Boris sniffed. 'She's only human, Catherine.'

Catherine's arm was tugged and she turned to see the garish orange twirls she had spent the better part of a week making atop the head of the woman in question. Virginia's eyes were bright underneath the headdress. Catherine wondered momentarily if it were really as necessary to fight age with make-up as Virginia did. She banished the thought and embraced her friend.

'Ah, my dear! You wear it so well.'

'That's what everyone's telling me and thank you for it. I love it.'

Catherine gestured to Boris. 'Virginia, this is Boris Shakhovskoy.'

Virginia shook Boris' large hand. 'Hello, thank you for coming.' She turned to Catherine. 'Your lover?'

'He's too good for me. My barman, usually.'

'Hope for me yet, then. Oh, here's the opening.' Virginia gestured to the doors at the back of the hall. The rugged-up people – despite the heaters, no one had removed a coat – started passing by them into the theatre space. Virginia took a big breath and shook her face, her mouth open, as if she was warming up to go onstage. 'Here goes nothing. They've just made changes to the running order in the last thirty minutes. These girls love to keep me on my toes.' She winked lasciviously at Catherine and walked in.

Catherine and Boris fell into step. He smiled wanly. 'Do you get that much?'

Catherine sipped her rapidly disappearing drink. 'What?'

'The low level sexual harassment.'

Catherine considered the question. 'More from men than women, and more from people who don't buy my hats than the precious few who do.'

'It must get you down.'

Catherine let a child in a wheelchair move in front of them. 'There are worse things in the world, but yes, it's tiresome. Sometimes it's appalling what people think they can get away with.'

In a few minutes they had moved inside with the throng. Catherine had the sense Boris had more to say, but the lights flickered. The stage was set up with the audience in bleachers erected especially around the constructed circus ring. Heaters around the room were still burning, but they may as well have been candles in Antarctica. Catherine pulled her coat closer and considered putting on her gloves.

They found seats in the middle row just on the aisle. Catherine looked at her empty glass and wondered about intermission, then chided herself for being so focused on the easy joys of booze when people were about to take risks for her pleasure.

Conversations around them died as the lights dimmed.

The show began in darkness. A single voice sang a low note which rose slowly in pitch until it flipped into a shuddering high note, just beyond the singer's range. When it broke into falsetto, a second voice joined in, mimicking the aural trajectory. This was repeated with four other voices, until the stage was filled with breaking notes and harsh cries. It gave a sense of panic, a futile grab at beauty that was foiled and yet familiar. All too human. The hair stood up on Catherine's neck. Boris leaned forward, mesmerised.

The sound built in volume until it hit a crescendo that broke into a wail. From offstage a drum boomed and the lights came up to show the six performers, again in the human pyramid formation. Catherine's hands came together unbidden, joining the rest of the audience in thunderous applause. The topmost performer rolled and fell through the air. Spinning, with her red ponytail a helicopter of colour flying before she landed on her feet. The others melted their way down the human structure with a grace that made Catherine think, 'oh yes, that just how humans move,' even though she knew otherwise.

'Welcome,' the lead performer called. She was shorter than the others, but held herself with power; her muscular body rippled in the purple and black of her leotard. A Bowie-esque lightning bolt was painted on one side of her face in a red that matched her hair. A spotlight shone on her as the rest of the stage again darkened.

'Welcome to *Warped*. Tonight we will push ourselves to the limits of our bodies, to help you push the limits of your mind.' She stood almost completely still. Catherine was aware of movement behind her, but could not break eye contact with this woman. 'Usually we would say don't try this at home. But at this late stage of climate change, we say "give it a whirl".'

Catherine smiled as Boris snorted.

The performers were grouped in two lines perpendicular to the front of stage. A wide spotlight shone on the performer at the front of each line as they started a low chant.

The broader light illuminated two lengths of material that hung from the roof, one purple, one black. The sound of rock and roll now augmented the chanting and singing and the six acrobats began dancing in a circle while one of the lengths of cloth started moving. Catherine at first thought the purple material was being manipulated from below and strained to see how, then noticed, at almost the roof top, the woman entwined within the material. Tissu, Virginia called it, a French word, though the French called them aerial silks.

The performer spread an arm and a leg as wide as they could, elongating the horizontal pose, before bringing their right hand slowly up and then, crashing it down. A flurry of movement followed as the performer fell with gravity, spinning in the unfurling tissu in exaggerated, seemingly unstoppable motion.

Boris gasped beside her as the acrobat's legs tumbled, circling, before stopping, just a metre from the ground. Catherine cheered, unbidden, as the acrobat unwound themselves from the tissu and made a small bow, before gesturing to the opposite tissu.

Catherine was unsurprised to see another acrobat in the rafters as the music changed pitch to something more eerie. This performer had no preamble, but spun into what at first appeared an identical fall, but quickly morphed into a wider armed tumble. Again, the hair on Catherine's neck stood on end.

Boris called out again as the performer twisted. The troupe below stopped their singing. One cried, 'Sil!' A matching cry came from the first woman who had fallen.

Catherine looked to her, as eyes wide, she clutched the material from which she had descended. Catherine followed her gaze to the swiftly tumbling performer. A hand was now visible, reaching out from her body for purchase on silk, or anything. Four more metres to the ground. Two metres. Her arm waving.

She stopped abruptly.

The crack was audible above the backing music.

Everyone heard it. Just as they saw the acrobat's sudden stop. The crowd gasped as one. While the first acrobat's tissu was stretched at a 40 degree angle, held taut by her hand, this newly fallen acrobat, entwined in black ribbon, hung limply. Her feet were a metre from the ground. Her head was caught in the silk at an angle impossible for survival.

As Catherine's eyes bugged, she became aware that all the performers had stopped, even as the music played on. Faces turned to strangers, looking for answers. Was this part of the show? Horror mirrored back as all came to the conclusion that it was not. The sound of anguish rose around her as all eyes returned to the performer's body, resting at the angle of a hanged prisoner. Boris's face was completely pale. He stared back at her. Disbelieving. Knowing.

Any last hope died when the music stopped, abruptly, mid-tune.

People stood in their seats. The performers scattered, three running off stage and three towards the woman entangled in the black material. A dark haired woman with a streak of grey ran from the front seats, yelling 'Jean! Is that Jean?', only for another performer to run towards her and embrace her.

Catherine supposed when there was that much make up, not recognising your own daughter was more than forgivable.

'No, it's not Jean,' Catherine whispered, her eyes transfixed on the suspended woman.

The house lights came up as technicians ran out, Virginia with them, her face almost completely white in the stark light. They were all looking up at the dead – surely dead – performer. Virginia turned, making brief eye contact with Catherine. She held up her hands. Amazingly, considering the circumstances, people stopped moving.

'There has been an accident. An ambulance has been called.' She turned her head as the tissu started lowering on a pulley. Virginia's hand went to her chest and she convulsed once, inhaling quickly and steadying herself.

'Please leave us for tonight. We will discuss refunds in due course.

I'm so sorry.' Her voice was dry, hoarse. She opened her mouth to say more, but she could not.

After a few seconds absorbing the information, the crowd moved as one, slowly, as if dumbstruck at the sight.

Catherine felt she should be doing something else, but didn't know what. With the sounds of breathing and a few sobs in the air, she and Boris walked slowly away with the crowd. She was holding his hand. She wondered when that had happened.

As she came to the door, she turned to view the stage once again. The body was now lying across the ground, still wrapped in the material. The crowd at the door parted for two paramedics to enter, their hands covered in blue gloves and their faces calm. They didn't make eye contact, but resolutely strode into the scene. Catherine blinked at them gratefully, and wondered, if not Jean, who had fallen?

Thirty almost silent minutes later, Catherine sat at the Brunswick Green and Boris was putting a double gin in front of her. The inside was packed and so Catherine had sat outside where only a few smokers dared, huddled close to the gas heater beside her. Post another shower, the wind swirled overhead. Catherine nodded at the weather's rare showing of appropriate mood. As Boris sat, Catherine's phone chirped.

'Who's that?'

Catherine blinked. 'It's Virginia. Why the hell is she texting me?'

'I don't know. I text you when something goes wrong. She probably doesn't know what to do with herself.'

She read the message again. 'The woman's name was Silver.'

'To Silver.' Boris raised his pint slightly and drank deep.

They sat in silence for several minutes. Catherine drank fast, then watched the plants drip the last of the rainwater onto each other. She thought about the nature of gravity and whether one day she could watch rain fall on another planet.

'What are you thinking about?' Boris asked. She told him.

'Space tourism. Nature docos from beyond Earth?'

Boris leaned back, happy to be distracted. 'It'll probably be just a camera set up on Titan or something, just a channel on the telly.'

There was another long silence. All thoughts came slowly. 'Does it rain there?'

'Probably not, but it probably rains hydrogen somewhere, or is it nitrogen?'

'Anyway, I was just thinking about rain falling softer on a planet with less gravity.'

'Maybe you're sensitive about gravity because of Silver.'

Catherine nodded and drained her glass. 'Do people die there?'

Boris spoke quietly. 'You're seeing death in places we haven't found life yet. Is that anthropomorphising?'

'You mean death might not be universal?'

'I've never met a dead Martian. Still, you're empty.'

Boris got up to go to the bar but Catherine stopped him. 'I'm going home. I just can't stop hearing it.'

Boris nodded, looking up a long second. 'That gravity will get you every time.'

2

The rain might be cold, but I only notice because I'm living.
~Ciara Beretta

To the evening eye, mornings have something like the romance of a well-trodden dance, which pushes humans through varying elevations of consciousness – but in the moment, most people are too busy thinking about bed, and work, and children, and caffeine, to appreciate it.

Most mornings are barely registered, as human existence goes. No one really notices the mundanity of the alarms, the sheets, the hallways. This is especially true for those who live alone. The more community you have around you, the more you pay attention to mornings. Ask anyone in an overcrowded prison.

Catherine wasn't in prison – not yet, as she regularly said.

Catherine was aware of Silver's death the moment her eyes fluttered open. She was aware of the light in her room and the weight of her cat on her legs. A rhythm in her breath seemed eternal but wasn't, so she listened to it and wondered if it were more beautiful or not because one day it would be silenced. Outside there had been rain, she could tell by the sound of the cars on the road, though no water tapped on the roof. Catherine thought that was a shame. It should rain for weeks after a tragedy.

With both feet on the ground, she knew the day was supposed to be filled with hats, and at least two measuring sessions. Even at this early stage, there were strong feelings on both sides of her brain for chucking the day. Summer Catherine wanted to dance and make things because she had little time and dammit there were just too many songs to dance to. Winter Catherine felt cold and sad and couldn't stop thinking about the sound of a snapping neck.

She breathed deeply. This argument could wait for at least a coffee and a shower. Maybe in fifteen more minutes. Catherine closed her eyes and imagined being perfectly melted cheese.

A mere eight minutes later, her phone rang. Catherine snorted into her pillow, swearing in French. Why is it any moment of meaningful reflection on this planet is always interrupted by another bloody *homo sapien*? The curse of a social species.

Catherine moved to silence the damned thing only to see the caller's name: Virginia.

The day after a death in your circus, you're afforded some luxuries, like an answered call.

'Virginia, are you okay?

'Catherine, they're here.' Virginia's voice was querulous and faint.

'Who's that?'

'The police.' Virginia was breathing very quickly.

'Oh.' Catherine was sitting up now. 'Okay. That's confronting, but why's that a surprise?'

'They asked me questions and they've looked around the training space. Now they're going to the performance space. Oh Christ, this is too much.'

'Are you under arrest?'

'No. Not yet.' The "yet" flew upwards in pitch like it had been shot out of a cannon.

'Do they have a warrant?'

'No.'

Catherine shifted her weight, swinging her legs off the bed. 'Virginia, they would just be preparing a report for the coroner. Do you have anything to hide? Just yes or no.'

'Oh no, of course not.'

'Then offer them coffee and stop worrying.'

'I haven't slept.'

'I'm not surprised. I'm so sorry this has happened. I can't stop hearing the crack.'

'I know, I know. Me neither.' She paused. 'Catherine, I–'

'Yes?'

'What if it wasn't an accident?'

Catherine stood up. 'What makes you say that?' Virginia didn't immediately answer. Catherine cleared her throat. 'Actually, don't answer that. I'm coming over. With Boris.'

'Why?'

'Because you just said that, and if you're thinking that, you need me to help you unthink it.'

There was a pause on the other end of the call. 'Okay. I'd like that. Thank you.'

Catherine looked across at her wall of photos, grounding herself with the faces of people she loved, among them Britt Houden. 'Oh, Virginia, are they plainclothes or in uniform?'

'Uniform.'

'Right, so they aren't Homicide, they're just cops preparing a report and doing their job.'

'Ah, yes.'

Catherine's shoulders slumped. 'I'm going to come to you anyway, but keep a lid on the stress.'

Forty seven seconds later, Catherine's kettle was on, she was wearing her dressing gown and she had changed the ear she was holding the phone to.

'Mmm.'

'Boris.'

'Mmm.'

'I need you.'

'Mmm.' The noises were a crescendo of grumpy on Boris' side of the conversation.

'Virginia's worried last night wasn't an accident, or it might seem it.'

'Mmm?' Questioning now.

'Come on, dear, you stopped being a teenager an embarrassingly long time ago to still be grunting through conversations.'

Catherine looked out the window, towards his house about a kilometre away. She couldn't see it of course, but the sky was a beautiful picture of bleakness. It would rain again soon.

Boris spoke. 'How–' He cleared his throat. 'How do you know I wasn't eloquent and charming as a teen?'

'I suspect you were most days, after midday. Come on now, I need extra eyes. It's probably a wild goose chase, but she paid a hell of lot for that hat.'

'I'll be there in twenty.'

'Make it thirty, you need a shower. I'm trying to enjoy the little things of life today. You unshowered is a big thing that no one enjoys.'

He did shower, and felt almost human for it. Thirty three minutes later he watched Catherine moving her feet so as not to step in whatever it was below the passenger seat of his car. It remained the usual science experiment of a person perpetually with something better to do than clean a car. He saw he'd won points, however, for the two steaming Keep Cups full of coffee that sat in the tray between them.

'So we're going to the performance space?'

'No, the rehearsal space. Pascoe Vale. The performance space is still being looked at by the police. We go there, we annoy police. Headache all round. They've already been to the rehearsal space.' As she spoke, she pointed the direction for him to drive. 'I suspect we won't find much. I want to see what's got Virginia so worried that she's saying it might not be an accident.'

'She's feeling guilty about something.'

'I didn't know Silver at all, and I'm feeling guilty about watching her die.'

Boris turned the wheel, focusing on the road as the rain started again. He'd had a coffee, he knew – he'd been there as he drank it – but sometimes there was no effect. He was considering dabbling in Class A drugs when Catherine spoke.

'How long has the car been making that noise?'

'What noise?'

She pointed towards the front of the car. 'That whine? There, every time you accelerate.'

He sniffed. 'I dunno, maybe a week?'

'Could be time to see the mechanic.'

Boris groaned. 'My mechanic just retired.'

'So?'

'Well, I don't know any other ones.'

Catherine brought a hand to her chest. 'Oh no. The only mechanic in Melbourne just retired? How could this happen!' She shook her fist at the pale grey ceiling of the Ford Laser GL. 'Where do we protest? Brunswick Town hall? Spring Street? Canberra? I don't think we'll make it there by the sound of your engine, but this is important, right?'

'Weren't you trying to enjoy the little things today?' Boris rubbed his face.

'I am, dear. This is a highlight.'

The engine made a higher whine. Boris harmonised with a baritone sigh.

'It's pretty easy, Boris, just ask your friends who a good mechanic is and get their number. Even you can handle that.'

'Yep. I will.' Boris moved his cold leg closer to the heater see if it could feel anything again.

Ten minutes later, they arrived.

'Here it is, just in next to that computer firm.'

They pulled up. Boris' engine sounded grateful as the whine subsided.

'Oh my God.'

Catherine had barely exited the car before she was engulfed by Virginia, who sobbed and held her just above the waist. More low-level sexual harassment.

Catherine looked to Boris for support. He was quietly closing his car door and obviously not making eye contact. Catherine could see he was trying not to laugh; another minute and he would grow dimples. Typical, she thought. Call harassment out to me, ignore it when it happens.

Catherine tapped the woman's hideous green cardigan. 'Virginia, it's okay.'

Virginia wailed, 'It's so horrible.'

Her orange hair was getting up Catherine's nose. 'I know.'

'They'll ruin me.'

'They won't.'

'I'm so lonely in this.'

'Please Virginia, it's starting to rain.' That was no lie. A slick drizzle had started and cold water was irritating the base of Catherine's neck as she tried to gently push the woman off her.

Boris passed them and went into the open building. The heaters had been on for some time and Boris felt the warmth on his face even as he entered. Outside, Virginia and Catherine were still in their embrace. Boris waved to Catherine, enjoying her grimace a little too much.

The hall was a converted factory. Four massive steel bars dominated the overhead, running parallel from east to west. There was minimal carpeting, only a few metres that stopped at the fenced-off training area, where mats covered concrete. On the mats were all manner of stands, and hoops, rings and trapezes hung from the middle two overhead bars. Fifteen metres beyond them was the long flowing material. Tissu, Catherine had called it. French for fabric.

Boris wondered why there were heaters on here when no one was around. They glowed an orange that seemed completely out of place, inside or out, on a day like this. Perhaps they'd been switched on for the police.

Virginia was holding Catherine up outside. Boris spied the lockers on the other side of the mats. One of the doors was open. He walked across, knowing from the sound of Virginia's dramatics that Catherine wasn't even close to joining him.

The space was light, even with the poor weather outside, and smelled better than any gym he'd spent time in. Boris looked through the lockers, the initials marked on each. He checked for an S, and wondered what Silver's surname was. There were three S's. He tried them at random, and while the first two were locked, the third swung open. He found blue ribbons, a water bottle and a small doll that looked like it was juggling. Then he noticed the open locker on the end. A silver star was tacked beside the initials M.B. Inside it was a jar of what looked like tea. He didn't touch it.

Then he thought about it why he didn't, and he shoved politeness aside. He pushed his hand into his sleeves and brought out the jar in his cloth-covered fingers. He opened the spring lid, took a deep breath and almost coughed at the smell. Earl Grey it was not. The pungent dry leaves reminded him of mud, stagnant water and swimwear forgotten in the boot of a car. He flipped the lid closed and was just putting the jar back into the locker when Catherine walked in with Virginia.

'What the hell are you doing?'

Boris smiled his sweetest. 'Looking.'

Virginia's voice had gone from pathetic to powerful. Boris could almost feel his armpits start to sweat. 'Why?'

Catherine spoke firmly. 'Because that's what we do.'

After a haughty, silent three seconds, this set off another round of weeping from Virginia. Catherine looked like she was wondering where her cyanide was. Boris didn't roll his eyes, didn't smirk, and promised himself a beer with dinner. He was getting better. Then he remembered that someone had died and got back to looking.

Catherine tried to pull the woman upright. 'Virginia, you remember Boris.'

Virginia sniffed and looked Boris up and down. 'Yes I remember.' She turned to Catherine, leaning on her shoulder as she spoke out the side of her mouth. 'Good morning Boris. I'm sorry I yelled. I'm not at all myself today.'

Boris nodded, looking at Catherine as Virginia was clearly not going to make eye contact with him. 'Not at all. Last night must have been horrible for you. I'm so sorry for your loss.'

Virginia nodded, tears flowing down her face.

'Perhaps we should talk about what's worrying you and then we can know what we're looking for,' Catherine prompted.

A quarter of an hour later they were ensconced in Virginia's office, which was somehow colder than the massive training space. Boris and Catherine were sitting around her coffee table, which was very close to her desk, but also close to her coffee machine. Virginia sat on her purple couch holding Catherine's hand and recovering from more crying. Boris sat on a nearby armchair, and, uncharacteristically for him in this situation, was leading the conversation.

'How many in the troupe?'

'There are seventeen of us. But only seven were in the show. It's the most successful all-woman troupe in the southern hemisphere.'

Catherine decided not to ask how she quantified that and pursued her current thought. 'Are the cops interested in the whole troupe or just those in the show?'

'They wouldn't say.' Virginia was staring at her coffee cup as if it might bite at any second.

Catherine smiled. 'That's a good sign then. I think you're worrying about the wrong things here. There was a death, so they assist the coroner. I don't think they're looking to investigate you unless there's been–' she paused, shrugged, '–I don't know, safety concerns.'

Boris cut in. 'What about WorkSafe? Are they involved?'

Virginia shook her head. 'Another thing to worry about. I'm sure they'll be involved, but they inspected everything last week before the show – standard for circus. Jesus. WorkSafe, police. Jesus.'

Catherine's voice was measured. 'I'm sure it's just procedure, but that does bring me to the point at hand. Why would you say last night wasn't an accident?'

Virginia's eyes flashed at Boris, which he found odd, as he hadn't said anything. 'Of course it was an accident. Why would you say otherwise?'

'I didn't. *You* did, which is why we're here. Boris and I don't keep secrets. You can trust him if you trust me.'

Virginia took a sparrow sip of her drink. 'I have no real reason to suspect anything. There are tensions in any artistic group. Circus requires collaboration above all, but that means the first rule is being able to collaborate with very difficult people.'

'Who's difficult in your group? Was Silver?'

'She was very talented.'

'I know, and her body is barely cold, but if you want us to pursue anything, then you have to give us the truth and quickly.'

Virginia stared at the steam that was limply rising off her coffee. 'She was talented, but easily led. Everyone in the group adores Harley, but Silver was beyond that. She was Harley's acolyte.'

'Harley? Tell me about her.'

'Her performing name is Harlequin, but when I met her she was called Stella. She's been training with us for three years, after a successful stint in the US. Came from Adelaide. She's extremely talented, but she knows it. Sometimes she can pull rank on the others.'

Boris leaned in. 'The redhead?'

Virginia nodded, not looking at either of them.

Catherine kept on. 'Any chance she was pulling rank with Silver and it went wrong?'

'No. Nothing like that. You would never endanger the show.' She looked away a second. 'It's just. I don't know, just petty things. In the lead-up to the show, Harley wasn't talking to half the cast half the time. She was the show's director as well as a performer.'

'Did she make the last minute change, then?'

'How–? Oh, I told you last night. Yes. She changed the running order. The silks fall was going to be later in the show.'

'That's interesting.'

Boris' eye wandered. A purple clock above Virginia's desk told him he would need to be at work in two hours. He looked at Virginia clutching Catherine's hand and was indignant that moments of his life were being eaten by Catherine placating someone who didn't actually seem to be in any trouble.

He was looking out the window when he saw a woman walking towards the building. She was tall and athletic. That much was obvious even though she wore a waist-length heavy black jacket over red tights. She walked as if she were held together by springs. Her honey blonde hair was tied up in a ponytail. What amazed Boris was how quickly she covered the ground between the corner and the building. She would be gone, Boris reckoned, in a further fifteen seconds, at which point he would have to go back to listening to Virginia trying to wail herself into Catherine's pants again.

The woman zeroed in on the training centre. Boris blinked and wondered if she'd been in the show the night before.

She walked in without knocking. She jolted to a stop as she saw Boris and Catherine.

Virginia greeted her. 'Ciara.'

'Who are these people?' She had a thick Mediterranean accent; her eyes were wide.

Virginia put down her cup. 'These are friends, Ciara. What's wrong?'

'Vee. The police called me.'

Virginia stood. 'Oh my God Ciara. I know. I gave them your number as you were the safety officer. I'm so sorry, I was in a flap and didn't text you.'

'Oh. You knew.'

Virginia stood and hugged the woman. Releasing her, she gestured to Catherine.

'Ciara, this is Catherine Kint. She's very clever and I think she could help us. This is Boris.'

Boris stood and shook her hand. It was warm despite the weather outside. Ciara held his gaze a moment and then turned as Catherine spoke.

'Boris and I were both at the show last night. I can't imagine what you're going through.'

'Grazie.' She seemed about to speak before she went very quiet. Boris was confused until he saw the tears running down her olive cheeks. He checked his pocket for a handkerchief. Nothing. He only seemed to have them when they weren't useful.

Ciara spoke though tears. 'Virginia, I'm sorry to come unannounced, I didn't know where to go.'

'Sit down, darling, I'll make you some tea. What did the police say?'

Ciara sat and took three long breaths. 'They didn't say much. Just asked me questions about the precautions and risk assessment, then I spoke about my relationship with Silver.'

'Oh, but that was a year ago.'

'They meant my professional relationship.' If Ciara was annoyed at Virginia's admission, it didn't show. 'I talked also about our friendship. About preparation for the show. Have they spoken to the other girls?'

'No, they only wanted the lead on the health and safety.'

She exhaled with her eyes closed. 'Oh. Okay.'

'I know. Just expect that WorkSafe will be in touch with you, too.'

'So the police, they talk to you too?'

Virginia sniffed and continued to hold her hand. 'Yes, they spoke to me. They left here about an hour ago. I was worried that we were being investigated, but Catherine knows about this and has assured me it's just routine.'

Ciara nodded. 'They asked if we had done this stunt much. I told them we had in the previous show, but that we changed the variations in the leg movements.' She turned to Boris. 'That was supposed to be a warm-up to the harder parts, when mine and Silver's routines would differ.'

'Oh,' Boris looked up. 'That was you on the other tissu?'

'Yes.' She nodded, tears again falling from her eyes. 'I knew what it was as soon as I heard the noise. I'll never stop hearing it.'

'I'm so sorry.'

'Don't be. It's Silver you should be sorry for.'

Boris touched her hand lightly. 'I have a lot of sympathy to go around.'

Catherine chipped in, 'I have a question. When someone does a trick like the one you did last night,' She gave a small smile to the two women, 'does someone help to wind you into the tissu?'

Ciara shook her head. 'No, we wrap ourselves.'

'Ok, just making sure there's no question of sabotage or foul play with the tissu itself.'

Boris couldn't place the look that Ciara was giving to Virginia. The older woman spoke, for the first time in a neutral way. 'Just tell them everything.'

Ciara rolled her shoulders. 'It's just that if Harley had died, maybe it would have been, as you say it, foul play.'

Catherine leaned back as Boris' demeanour changed. The man's brain had obviously shifted gears. A minute earlier he'd been almost asleep; now his knees, toes and nose all indicated his full attention was on Ciara.

Catherine removed Virginia's hand from her knee as Ciara spoke again. Virginia was so bad at taking a hint she reminded Catherine of a man, an insult she didn't give lightly.

'I was going to leave after this run,' said Ciara

Virginia gasped audibly. Ciara nodded and continued talking. 'There are always some small issues in a circus, but here it was disaster. Harley has everyone on strings, and was only challenged by me.'

'I'm sorry you felt that. She was the show's director though. She had authority.' Virginia's voice was tighter than a noose. Her voice became more full-bodied, as if trying to trump against Ciara's soft accent. Outside, thunder rolled and Boris shivered.

Ciara started crying. After a second, Virginia joined in. Boris and Catherine made eye contact and had their own silent thoughts on death as they waited it out. In a while, Virginia spoke. 'I'm sorry you didn't feel I was in control of the group, Ciara.'

'I don't blame you, Vee. She is so good at what she does. She changed things so much.'

'What do you mean?' Catherine asked.

Ciara smiled. Catherine thought it was a fragile smile, it seemed to flicker. 'Have you ever met someone who talks to you and makes you feel like you're the only person on Earth? And seconds later,' she snapped her fingers, 'they forget your name?'

Virginia bristled. 'That's unfair.'

'You can talk later. You said we could trust these people.' Ciara bunched the hand that wasn't holding her tea into a ball, an action that did not escape Catherine or Boris. 'You can call her the big personality, you can call her diva. But she's someone who is good at two things: circus and making people feel like nothing.'

'How did she get on with Silver?' Boris asked.

'They were best friends, according to both of them. I think Silver was just so in love she would do anything for Harley. They met in New York, before they came back here. Silver said Harley made her feel okay about not getting work over there.'

'And how do you think Harley felt?'

Ciara was on the point of tears again. 'Boris, it is Boris, correct?' He nodded. 'I don't think that woman feels anything.'

A moment's silence followed. Boris expected Virginia to speak or cry, but she just looked at her hands.

'So Harley was the Director, she chose the routine you would do?' he continued.

'No, Silver and I had written the routine. We brought it to Harley two months ago.'

'Tell me about the tissu, Ciara,' said Catherine. 'Was that trick hard?'

'Not really. It look spectacular, but it's just falling really, then catching.'

'So Silver would have done it before?'

'A thousand times.'

'How did you get up there, at the top of the ribbons?'

'By the *sartiame*, uh,' her hand trembled in the air before her. 'The word, um, rigging.'

'Did she seem okay when she was going up?'

Ciara blinked twice. 'Yes. She was pumped. The show was everything to her.'

'Not you?'

'What?'

'You said the show was everything to *her*. Did you leave yourself out of that?'

'No. The show is everything that matters to everyone in our troupe.' She was matter of fact. As if it didn't have to be said.

Boris left twenty minutes later to get to work. As Ciara made more tea, Virginia took Catherine quietly aside.

'Your man. Is he good?'

'He's the best.'

'You know, you could do so much better. You're beautiful.'

'I told you last night, it's not–'

'So much better.' Virginia was standing close, too close. Catherine knew death was an aphrodisiac, but that often made sleazy people seem even worse than they usually were.

Her face couldn't have been more neutral had it been tattooed with a Swiss flag, but she let a little steel into her voice. 'Boris and I work together and occasionally he saves my life. I couldn't do better, even if he was my lover.'

'Oh.'

3

Give me a lever long enough and a place to stand, and I will walk away, make a hat, then go dancing.
~Catherine Kint (and Archimedes)

As Boris drove away, the rain went from hard to diabolical. The windscreen wipers worked overtime and he craned his neck, as if that would help him see through the downpour. He glanced at the clock: 11:37. He could have stayed longer, but this rain would have made him late. Catherine could take it further. Perhaps she could spend the whole day with Ciara. Perhaps they'd get coffee and ice cream and walk home together in the rain.

Boris blinked once, twice.

'A woman died, and you're getting pissy about Catherine spending time with a pretty person. Get a grip fella.' He shook his head at himself then peered through the rain. Thirty seconds later he spoke again, quietly. 'You didn't make a fool of yourself. Just chalk that up as a win, okay?'

He sighed. There were times when he wished he could have a holiday as someone else.

The traffic was somehow moving easily along Royal Parade. Most of the smart money must have seen the weather coming. Boris blinked as he saw someone inexplicably walking on the median strip between the tram lanes and the bike lane. Boris did a quick mirror check and pulled to the side of the road. He wound the window down.

'Hey, want a lift?'

The figure looked up. She was tall, with thick dark hair, plastered to her face.

'I'm right.' She broke eye contact and held a hand up in a "no".

'Are you sure? It's pissing down. I could–' He paused. 'Take you to a tram stop, or the shops down the road. At least you'll be out of this.' As he spoke, the rain increased in intensity.

The woman turned. Looked at Boris, then squinted at the sky. She looked miserable, but unbowed.

Boris continued. 'Hey, see that stick?' It was a fallen branch, about sixty centimetres long and the thickness of a pool cue. She looked at it, and back to him.

'You can bring that and sit in the back. If I'm a psycho, you can hit me with it.'

The woman ran a hand over her face, thinking. Picked up the stick and ran over. As she approached the car, she looked at the stick and threw it away.

She got into the front seat.

'Thanks,' she said frostily.

'No problem.' Boris turned the heater up and drove, keeping his whole body as far from hers as possible. 'Um, sorry about the mess.'

The woman smiled thinly. 'It's a dry mess at least.'

Thunder cracked almost on top of them and they both jumped. 'Shit.'

The woman was breathing deeply. 'Oh,' she said quietly.

'Um, where can I take you?'

'Just a tram stop.'

'Sure, I'm heading up Sydney Road as far as the Glasgow Palace if that's helpful. I'm Boris, by the way.'

'Hi, Boris. Could you drop me at Dawson Street?'

'Sure.' Boris thought about the radio. About the dank smell of his car. About how even two years ago he wouldn't have got the hint and would have asked her name. So much growth. He suppressed rolling his eyes.

The car made the whining sound again. 'Oh mate, you've got transmission issues.'

'I've what?'

'Your transmission. Can't you hear that?'

'Ah, yeah. It just sounds like my car needs to go to a mechanic to me. What's a transmission?'

She smiled. Even looking at the road, Boris could see her dimples. 'Not a car guy?'

'No, never learned.'

'Know what gears are?'

'Yep. Got that.'

'The transmission is what moves gears through on an auto. Yours is in strife. Or it could be something more expensive.'

'Shit. My mechanic just retired.'

She was quiet for a moment, looking out the window at the rain on concrete. 'Are you in a hurry?

Boris looked at the clock. 11:47. Thirteen minutes till work. 'Not hugely.'

'Take me a bit down Dawson Street, I'll show you a good mechanic.'

'Ok. Thanks. I can't leave it now though, I've got to work.'

'You work at the Palace?'

'Yep.' Boris exhaled through his nose.

'Cool.'

They drove in silence as he turned down Dawson and passed the Brunswick Baths. A family of four walked past them in bright towels, looking ridiculous in the rain.

'Boris?' She asked as they went over the train line.

'Yeah?'

'That thing you did, with the stick, when you knew I was worried you were a psycho?'

'Ah, yeah?'

'That was, nice, but kinda dumb.'

Boris shrugged. 'I know why someone wouldn't want to get in a car with a stranger. I know that women have been murdered around here. I hate it, but I understand. I just really didn't want you stuck in the rain.'

'It's here.' She pointed. A garage was on the left side, Boris pulled in. "Angelo's" read a neon sign. 'Come on Saturday morning. The best mechanic is on then.'

'Oh cool. I will.'

She held out a hand. 'I'm Jolene.'

Boris felt himself smiling a lot. 'Right. Nice to meet you.'

'Boris, did it occur to you that I might be a psycho?'

Boris was quiet a second. The rain was easing. 'Um, No. Plus, even if you were, it was really raining.'

'Right.' She smiled and got out of the car.

Boris looked at the clock. He had three minutes.

The thunder cracked again.

Boris was passing Catherine to check the ice when he heard her sigh.

'Boris, that's the third time you've gone past my empty glass this evening. What's got you so dreamy? Not just Ciara is it?'

Boris blanched and reached for her glass. 'I'm a bartender of a certain age on a very quiet Wednesday. I watched someone die last night. Forgive me a little ennui.'

'Forgiveness is easier with a beverage, Mr Sartre.' She tapped the bar twice. Another barfly giggled.

Boris reached for the bottle. 'So how far did you get?'

'Third base.'

'You're hilarious, you know that?'

Catherine stretched on her barstool. 'Just background really. Everyone seems to dislike everyone else, and people were mad at Virginia for not taking charge as CEO. It's not our beef though. I just wanted to help Virginia. She's painful, but she knows so many people who love my hats. As for what happened: let the cops be cops.'

Boris delivered the drink and took Catherine's resting credit card from in front of her. 'That does seem to be what normal people do.'

Boris nodded and wandered off. Catherine took a long drink, then cracked a knuckle. 'Would it wake you up if I said she may join me for a drink later?'

'Who?'

'Ciara. Why? Are you mooning about something else? This seemed your stock standard,' she raised one hand from her glass to make talking signs, '"Boris met a girl" induced hopelessness.'

Boris threw a tea towel over his shoulder haughtily, 'I don't recall ever being critical of you when you're in a bad mood.'

'Because I don't let it happen, dear. I'm simply trying to elevate you to my personal cloud of nirvana. Humans will go much further if they can open themselves to the wonders of the web without worrying about the spider.'

'You sound like a gin shaman. You should go back to Ocean Grove. I know this bloke.'

Catherine contemplated her glass, finding a smudge. 'Shush, dear. I'm simply teasing you and grateful that we don't have to do anything more about the unpleasant business of last night.'

The door opened with a ferocity, and there was Ciara, looking stunned. She staggered to the bar for support, blood smeared on her face. Several patrons stood as Boris nearly jumped the bar.

Ciara pushed herself up on her elbows and blood ran from her mouth. Catherine was upon her in a second.

'Ciara, what happened?'

'I got hit' she started, then fell back down. Catherine could see a bruise rising on the left side of her face.

'Call police and an ambulance, Boris.'

'No.' Ciara shook and her eyes widened, wet with tears. 'No police. No ambulance. Please, ugh, no police.' Her voice wasn't slurred, though she was clearly in pain.

Catherine and Boris helped her to a chair, Boris donating his tea towel to soak up the blood coming from her mouth. A throng of other patrons surrounded them at a two metre radius. Someone passed Boris a glass.

'Here, have some water,' he offered.

'Bring me bourbon please. Neat. Double. And some ice, please.'

Boris turned back to the bar. While pouring, he heard Ciara's accented tones assuring the company, 'I'm okay. Please everyone, let me speak to Catherine.'

Catherine and Ciara retreated to the relative privacy of the bar nook in the northeast corner. Boris gave Jamie – who had knocked off – a meaningful look and Jamie put down his pint and returned to the business side of the bar.

Boris placed the bourbon in front of Ciara and sat on the other side of her to Catherine. Ciara's hand shook until she steadied it by holding the glass.

'What happened?' Catherine asked.

'After I got off the train, I was walking up that street.' Ciara pointed to the window over Albion Street across the room. 'Someone whistled at me. I didn't look. I walked here and then I felt hands on me. There was no one around but him. I yelled. Two fists hit my head. One here' she pointed to her left check. 'And one here, she touched above her hairline.'

Boris couldn't see blood against her dark blonde hair. He could smell her hair and tried to ignore how much he liked it.

'I fell. I thought I would die. I kicked out with my foot and caught a leg. I was waiting for the kicks to come at me. But nothing. He was gone.'

Catherine leaned in. 'It was a man?'

'Yes. Wearing black. A rain jacket. Swishy sounds while he hit me. Shorter than Boris.'

'Did he say anything?'

'To shut up.' She breathed out slowly. Took a sip. 'It was, grab, shut up, bang bang, fall, kick. Then he spoke once more and was gone.'

'What was the last thing?'

'We're watching.'

Jamie cut in from the bar. 'Boris, I gotta go. My date's here.'

'What the–?' Boris shook his head. 'All right man. Thanks.' He hauled himself off the bar stool and picked up Ciara's empty glass. 'I'll get you another.'

Catherine's voice followed him as he walked to the bar.

'Boris?'

'Yes, you too Catherine.'

As Jamie opened the door to leave, a blast of cold air made Boris' skin goosebump.

Boris tended the bar. He watched the women talk, knowing that if he went to them, someone would want a drink. He did his job, knowing Catherine would do hers. It grated, because he wanted to help. If he closed his eyes he heard the crack of Silver's neck, then Ciara's crying from earlier.

'Two pots of Coburg and a sav blanc.'

'Three pints of Hawkers.'

'Do you do hot chips at this time, mate?'

'Three bourbon and cokes.'

'Change for the pool table, Boris?'

Closed his eyes. *Crack*.

Ciara drank two bourbons. The first evaporated in front of her, the second lingered. With Ciara breathing more slowly, Catherine spoke the question that had been with her for twelve minutes.

'You've done nothing wrong and you've been assaulted. Why not involve the police?'

Ciara shook head slowly and deliberately. 'I don't feel comfortable'

'That's when you go to police.'

'Please, Catherine. Today, they talk to me about death, maybe murder. My friend's murder. They see a silly girl with a funky accent. I don't expect help. Only trouble.'

Catherine thought of that. Thought of some of the cops she'd known. Thought about all the racism she'd never experienced.

'Why do you think you were hit?'

Ciara shrugged. 'Unlucky. Maybe they want my bag.'

'Did they go near your bag?'

Ciara shook her head.

Catherine put just a touch of steel in her voice. 'No, and they said they were watching. There isn't time to play dumb, Ciara.'

Boris had lit the tea candles an hour earlier. Their soft flicker was doing its job, calming the room and taking the sting out of the light. Ciara was quiet. Catherine watched Ciara carefully, wondering if she'd run at the challenge.

'He didn't want my bag. It was a message.'

'From Harlequin?'

'I think so.' Ciara's nose wrinkled and she brought the glass to her mouth without sipping.

'Tell me everything you did today.'

'What? I was with you.'

'I know, but only until one. What happened after? What would someone see if they were watching?'

Ciara did take a sip, now. Catherine followed suit then ordered another round with her eyes. Boris was suddenly a good barman again and he moved quickly. Ciara spoke just as he reached for the lime.

'I left you and went to go to work. I work in a cafe in town. I walked to the station and realised I just–' she made a movement with her hand, 'so I called and said I was sick. Then I walked to a park. I sat for a long time. It rained. I didn't care. Then I was cold so I walked. I walked to her house and looked at it. I wanted to see her face in the window.' A tear ran down her face. 'There was no one there. I smoked a cigarette and went home. I ate. I rang my Mama. I lay down and tried to sleep. I didn't sleep. I put my coat back on and came to find you.'

Boris put the two drinks in front of them, making eye contact briefly with both before staring behind them at the rain that was coming in so hard it was streaking down the windowpanes.

Catherine put her fingers around the chilled glass that held her gin and tonic. 'I think it's because you were at her house.'

'What?'

'It's a guess. But I'm trying to think why anyone would hit you.'

Ciara's face was showing more of the bruise now. Boris had noticed too and brought over another tea towel with ice in it.

'You must realise, dear. When you hit someone, you take a risk. Because they may hurt you back, or you may get caught.' She took a sip; Ciara listened closely. 'So why would someone take this risk? All I can think is that someone is worried about you finding something out, and the only thing you did today was look at Silver's house.'

'What are you thinking?'

'I think tomorrow you should go there again.'

'Why? What if I'm hurt?'

'You won't be. Because you'll have Boris with you.'

They both looked over at Boris, who was pouring a glass of wine. The tea towel hanging off his jeans was about to fall onto the bar floor.

'What will he do?' Ciara asked.

Catherine turned back to the woman. 'I think we should have a look in there. Aren't you a little curious?'

'I don't know what I would be looking for.' She bit her lip. 'If Harley had done something she won't have left a note explaining herself there. She is not a crazy person.'

Catherine leaned back in her seat. Perhaps the gin was making her think poorly. It had to happen on occasion. 'Maybe it wasn't her. Maybe there's nothing. Maybe it was an accident. So why the cloak and dagger?'

'The what?'

'Why follow you, why hurt you?'

'I don't know if Harley did kill my Silver. But I know she would do anything to hurt me.'

My Silver. Catherine banked those words and kept going. 'Why?'

'I know her true nature. She is a scorpion. She can only hurt people.'

Catherine thought she saw lightning, but it was only a passing tram's antennae sparking against the electric wire, brighter in a dark night. The rain wasn't so heavy now.

Ciara took a thoughtful sip, then curled her lip and pushed the drink away.

'Harley was the first girl to talk to me. When I joined the group. She was so friendly. And so talented. What she can do with hula hoops is like nothing you know.'

'You were impressed.'

'I was impressed, and relieved. I didn't know anyone. I am just a girl from Sicily and I came to the other side of the world. She made me feel so welcome. That night we went dancing.'

She stroked her nose and Catherine could see a tear welling. She wanted to reach out and touch Ciara's hand, but didn't in case that made it worse.

'I didn't know where we were. I was new in town, and quite drunk. I remember she said she was going for more drinks, and she never came back. I looked, but she was a ghost.'

She smiled, wiped her eyes. 'I called, I called again. Nothing. I only had one number in all of Australia. It was winter like this. I walk for two hours to get home. The next days she wouldn't speak to me.'

'Did you do something to annoy her?'

'That's what I thought, but she never said. Then I found out, months later. She wanted me to feel helpless so I knew my place in the circus.' She drank the bourbon, all of it. 'She's a fucking bitch.'

Catherine breathed in. She knew stories like that, knew people like that. It still made no sense to her.

'So pecking order was a big part of the group culture?'

'Pecking order?'

'I think it's a chicken thing, like top dog. I don't know, I live here, not on a farm.'

Ciara nodded. 'Whoever is close to her, is top dog. Or second.' Her nose wrinkled. 'Virginia is supposed to be the lead, but it's hollow. She just pays us.'

Catherine's head turned as Boris put a chair seat down on the bar next to her. 'Good God, man, that time already? What about last drinks?'

He pointed at their glasses. 'That was them.'

'You need your vocals tested. I didn't hear a bloody thing.' She slapped her hands on her thighs. 'Right, we'll take this back to mine. I've already booked you for tomorrow, dear.'

Boris' eyebrow raised. 'Doing what?'

'A little b and e'

'What is b and e?' Ciara asked.

Boris looked around to see if anyone was in earshot. 'Breaking and entering.'

'No. We shouldn't' Ciara had another tear on her cheek.

Now Catherine did take her hand. 'Ciara, you lost a friend yesterday, you've been assaulted tonight and the police have asked you a lot of questions. You have every right to feel afraid.'

'I am. I also don't know what we would find there. And if the police found us…'

'We can be discreet. We only go with Boris, early morning, and he'll do the grunt work. You just walk through with me.'

'What will you do?'

'I'll notice things. When you were in a relationship with Silver, was it at that house?'

Ciara looked aghast, then blinked. 'I wondered if you heard that.'

'I did, and I noticed that you didn't mention it tonight. I'm only pointing that out to show you I notice things. It's what I do.' She checked herself. 'When I'm not making hats. Now, my place? It's just round the corner and we can brief Boris.'

Boris was hanging back, rubbing his beard. 'No pressure, you understand,' he said. His voice was soft.

Ciara stood suddenly. "I'm going to go home. I think I need to sleep.'

'Of course. Shall I call you a car?'

She shook her head. Not looking at them. 'No. I will walk for a bit.'

'Are you sure? You were assaulted tonight.'

She breathed deeply. 'If I show fear, it will become everything in my head. That's what the circus has taught me. So much of circus is laughter and curiosity conquering fear and rules. Tonight, I will walk. Look, it's stopped raining.'

Catherine looked up just as lightning flashed.

'If you're sure.'

'Call me before you arrive tomorrow. I need to think. Ciao, Boris.'

With a flash of the glass door, she was gone.

'Weird day.' Boris stretched. 'I'm off the clock. Your place? Or do you need sleep?'

'I feel there's far too much possibility around for me to sleep. My place.' She grabbed her red coat and contrasting brown scarf from the hat stand that stood by the door six months of the year. Catherine had often wondered where it disappeared to in the summer months, but today didn't seem to be the day to ask.

Despite the coat, she shivered as Boris locked the staff exit of the pub. She couldn't see a soul on Sydney Road, though most lights were on in the residential apartments on De Carle Street. A tram rattled past en route to town, three people on it. None looking happy.

They walked briskly, both keen to get their blood up and get out of the chill.

'Let's assume,' Catherine started, 'that something unpleasant is going on in the troupe. Someone is worried there's something to know, and wants to throw us off the scent. Take Ciara for example. She's brave in front of me, vulnerable in front of you. Somehow she knows what impresses us, then she's assaulted on the way to seeing us. Does this benefit her?'

She and Boris turned to Albion Street, taking in a further icy blast. He spoke carefully. 'I don't think she's full of shit.'

'Nor do I necessarily, but I'm playing devil's advocate. Say she is and she does this dance with us: why?'

Boris blew out his cheeks. 'We find out something that throws us onto a different scent. Or she's making sure we get involved, and involved in her. Sounds like this Harley person could have convinced us of something else.' He gesticulated but it was so cold he put his hand immediately back in his pocket.

Catherine pointed a finger. 'Maybe she wants us to find something out about the Harlequin lady.'

'Or she just wants us to get in the way of the truth ever coming out because we trip over our own feet?'

Catherine made a noise between a hum and agreement. 'That seems like something people who don't like us would say about us.'

They walked in silence for a few minutes, Boris keeping an eye out for potential attackers. It seemed silly that anyone would willingly stay in such cold conditions just to attack them. Occasionally, Boris liked that he wasn't that important.

Catherine clicked her tongue. 'Doesn't fit with me.'

'Me neither.' Boris agreed. 'I don't think we're that famous, and I think someone hit Ciara and we need to help her.'

'Yep. It doesn't make sense to me that you would bring more attention to a crime you did just in the hope that someone trips over someone else's feet. Still, I like that we have this level of critical engagement when it comes to helping people these days.'

'There's been growth, no question.'

Catherine's hands kept moving. 'I can get tied up once by a knife wielding maniac I thought needed help and quite happily forgive myself the next day. If it happens again though, I'll really have to give myself a solid talking to.'

Boris touched the scar near his eye. 'You'll have company there.'

They reached the door of Catherine's apartment. Her cat Minty was around her feet in no time, obviously keen to get inside.

'I thought you had a cat flap?' Boris began taking his coat off.

'I do. Sometimes she locks herself out. Plus it's one of the few times she ever really needs me.'

'It's nice to be needed I guess.'

Five minutes later, Catherine was on the floor in front of the coffee table and Boris was on the couch. Catherine's faux wooden gas heater was taking its sweet time taking out the chill. Boris was blowing on his hands between sips of his beer.

'She got attacked after visiting Silver's house. Why no cops then? Why not come back here? Why get so funny about us taking care of her? When she came to us?'

'Well, maybe she's had some poor experience with cops before,' said Boris. 'Why not come back here?' He rubbed his neck. 'Maybe she was tired and just had enough. She did lose a friend last night. Even if she had a hand in it, that would probably be a rollercoaster for anyone. As for the last bit, well. She's a circus performer, she's in grief, she seems like a feminist, and she's Italian?'

Catherine worked hard to not raise an eyebrow. 'Explain the feminist and the Italian part?'

'Italian, passionate people, big emotions. Naturally not all of them, but when you're discussing an Italian showing big emotions it doesn't seem racist unless you're saying they're lesser for it. Like saying because you're Anglo you're stoic and analytical, and that because I am Russian and Celtic I am tough and like a drink. The feminist thing was just about a likely independence that was championed by all waves of feminism, where you don't like asking anyone – police, and especially said tough Russian man – for help.'

'Ok, I'll pay that, but will get back to you about waves two and three of feminism.'

Boris picked up his beer. 'We don't have time for that now.'

'I'm simply filing for future discussion, my big Russo/Celtic friend. Personally, I thought you grew up in Reservoir.'

'I did, but felt the need to deflect my Aussieness in terms of that conversation.'

'Okay.' Catherine changed the topic. 'So tomorrow, a quick bit of break and enter?'

'Yes. You in?'

'Of course.' She looked at her drink. 'That just means this is my last for the night.' She sighed.

'Such things never crossed our mind years ago.'

'I don't recall making many plans for the next day years ago.'

He finished his beer. 'What do you think we'll find at Silver's house? Aside from potentially a bashing?'

'More than we would find sitting around here playing cards.'

'I can't fault your logic.'

4

Knowing how things work
is halfway to not fucking them up.
~Jolene Ardica

A few hours later, mist was fogging up Boris' car. Matched by the mist that was fogging up the entirety of Melbourne, which had blown a twenty five minute car trip out to forty. He and Catherine drove in milky darkness. The visibility was about twenty metres. Not dangerous, but you had to slow down. The sun would come up soon, but that would likely just change the hue of the fog; it wouldn't penetrate until later.

The glow of the streetlights gave the impression of driving through a cloudy dreamscape. Catherine thought of storm chasers, people who devoted their lives to following and documenting devastating weather events around the world. Surely there was a way of chasing fog, to see the night's emptiness coloured in by the mists and shapes of what seemed like a different, gentler dimension.

Despite the darkened beauty, the hour was early and Boris and Catherine spoke little as they drove to Ciara's flat, aside from Catherine chiding him on the state of his engine. She was quietly impressed that he was booked in for a service.

She moved her foot and realised another change.

'Did you clean up your car?'

'Just a little.' Boris tried not to sound defensive. Realised that he had failed miserably.

'Boris Shakhovskoy, are you in love with this woman?'

'It was time to tidy up, Catherine. Don't make it weird.'

A few seconds later she giggled and he groaned. They didn't speak again for ten minutes.

They circled the block where Ciara lived, twice. Neither saw anything out of the ordinary. Catherine texted Ciara that they were outside. A minute later, Ciara entered the car. She was ready, though she looked like she'd had even less sleep than Catherine and Boris. There was only the slightest sign of the cut by her eye. Either she had covered it with make-up, or she healed inhumanly fast.

'Good morning.'

'You get home okay?'

'No further problems. I couldn't sleep though. I'm not sure what we'll find at the house. I fear what I will find.'

'An object?' Catherine was surprised.

'No. I mean what I will feel.'

Catherine held a hand out to the back seat. Ciara took it. 'I'm sorry. I can't be much help for the feelings. Only that one day they will change.'

'Not today, though.' She spoke quietly.

'No, definitely not today.'

Boris changed the topic. 'Look at that cool purple car.' He pointed to a parked Fiat on the side street.

'Really Boris?'

'It's a great colour. Sorry, Ciara.'

'Don't be, Boris. That one is mine actually.'

'See.' Boris winked at Catherine. 'It's good to notice things, even on dark days. How does it drive, Ciara?'

'Some advice Boris?'

'Yeah?'

'Don't ever buy a car based on colour. It is impractical.'

'Thanks, that is totally something I would do.'

Once they arrived at the address Ciara gave them, they again grew vigilant. They drove around the block once, slowly. Ciara looked right, Catherine left. Neither saw anything of note, nobody loitering, nor did they see any police. A garbage truck rolled on in front and Boris took his time, not overtaking. Traffic was minimal, even this close to Flemington Road. Boris pulled over in a side street. Catherine and Ciara walked towards Silver's flat while Boris walked around the block from the opposite side, in case someone followed them in.

Catherine and Ciara moved in close to the building, a sixties concrete art deco knock-off. Popular in the inner west, for a reason Catherine didn't know and didn't care to. She checked her watch. 5:50am. An unnatural time to be awake at any stage of the year. So close to winter solstice it seemed bloody stupid.

'You have a key?' Ciara's voice broke into her thoughts. She looked at the blonde woman, seeing the last of her words as vapour blowing out of her mouth against the orange glow of the streetlight.

'No, I don't need one, but do you?'

'No.' She sniffed. 'I did once. A year ago.'

Catherine took out her hair pins and had the door open just as Boris lumbered up the driveway. Catherine shook off her last doubts and put one of her phone earbuds in her ear. She knew that he would be doing the same.

They moved inside, Catherine donning her gloves before she turned on the light.

Remnants of Silver's last meal were on the sideboard of the small kitchen. These apartments were cheap for their location – near the freeway – and their size. Catherine thought you would have to be some kind of contortionist to work in such a small kitchen.

'Just have a look around and let me know if anything seems out of place.'

'Si.' Ciara shook her head. 'I mean, okay.'

The kitchen was augmented by a living area and a small hallway led down to a bathroom and a bedroom. Double bed. A queen size would have left only centimetres for anything else. Nothing stood out immediately. Catherine took it slowly. Ciara stayed in the living area. Catherine checked the bathroom. Shower and toilet were clean. Some hair in the bathroom sink. No medicines in the cabinet, but some fungal cream, ibuprofen and mouthwash. Circus stars had the same issues as any athlete. Fungus and occasional halitosis. Catherine self-consciously ran her tongue over teeth. Yes she had brushed this morning, but that didn't guarantee fresh breath for late night drinkers.

The small window held candles in various states of use and a bottle of perfume endorsed by an actor Catherine didn't think much of. There may be a clue there, but it wasn't leaping out.

Catherine paused, struck not so much by a presence but an absence. Silver's house was devoid of photos. Not even one. In the living room was a framed poster of *Cirque de Soleil – Amaluna,* but this was the only decoration of any kind. There were no smiling photos of family, friends or lovers. It struck Catherine as emotionally Spartan.

Catherine returned to the kitchen. Ciara was sorting through papers on the small table.

'Anything?' Catherine's voice was low.

'I don't know what I am looking for.'

Catherine nodded, ignoring the usual drum in her gut that came from looking through other people's houses. 'Okay. Keep looking then.'

Catherine looked through the cupboards, amazed at the lack of liquor, but choosing not to comment on it. Nothing leapt out, though Silver was obviously a fan of teas and herbs.

'Was she into Chinese medicine?'

Ciara looked up. In the electric light of the kitchen, she appeared drawn. In the car Catherine hadn't noticed, but she looked tired to the point of swaying. Catherine tried to soften her tone.

'Ciara?'

Ciara blinked and came back to the world. 'Hello? Sorry.'

Catherine brandished a large jar of dark dried herbs. 'Was Silver into tea, or is this a Chinese medicine thing?'

Ciara took it and examined the label. 'Probably Chinese. Or Vietnamese. She was seeing a man in Sunshine. He was treating her.'

'Treating her for what?'

Ciara put down the papers. 'Sometimes she got tired.'

'That must be tough. Does he have a name?'

'Anderson?' Her brow knitted. 'No, Henderson or something. Something English.'

'There's a lot of English names in this country.'

'That's why I get confused.'

Catherine's phone vibrated in her ear. Ciara heard it and froze.

'Boris.'

'People coming. Don't look like cops. You have ten seconds if they're coming to the flat.'

Catherine looked up. The living room window's view didn't take in the driveway. She motioned Ciara to the bedroom. The Italian woman's eyes were wild. She walked down the hall quickly. Catherine could see the tension in her shoulders, but she made no noise.

There was no back door. Catherine hadn't given the bedroom a look-in yet, but saw there was no room in the cupboard for anything more than a rabbit.

Boris's voice in her ear. 'They're at Silver's door. They don't have a key and they really don't look like cops. Three people. Two men and a woman. One of the men and the woman look handy. I don't like my chances.'

'Got it. Don't engage. We'll try and get out the back.'

Silver's flat had a small balcony, with five iron rails running vertical between a top and bottom rung. It looked flimsy, but was strong when Catherine shook it. It was still dark outside; just a tinge of orange light on the fog. The drop, as far as Catherine could see, was about four metres. She breathed out. 'Jesus.'

Ciara moved in front of her. 'Do it like me.' She was over the iron rails in a second, and holding the top rung facing Catherine through the bars. She took a breath as there was a bang at the door.

'Like this, then.' She dropped and Catherine's voice caught. Ciara had grabbed the bottom rung and only her hands were visible. Her knuckles went white as her face came up. 'If we stay like this, we can listen.'

'You've got to be fucking joking.' Catherine breathed. She was aware of sweat on her neck. What Ciara had done looked about as easy as walking until you thought about doing it yourself. Then it became akin to flying.

'What?' asked Boris in her ear.

'Nothing. Move to the balcony.'

There was another bump at the door. Someone was getting in.

Catherine swung one leg over the rail and then the other. Rather than dropping, she gripped two vertical rails and slid down. Her arms told her exactly how long it had been since she had bothered with the gym. She looked at Ciara, whose eyes were closed. She was breathing easily and calmly. Catherine tried to match her. Underneath them, she heard Boris walking. She looked down and made eye contact with him. He was in position. He would break her fall. She knew he would. There was only a metre between her toes and his shoulders.

Voices in the apartment. She focused on them.

'Check the drawers, Tony.'

'Yep.'

'No dawdling. I don't want company.'

'She's dead, right?'

'The cops are alive. So's that dago bitch. If she's got something on me, it's not good.'

'I can't see anything suss.'

'Did you notice the fucking light was on? You reckon that's not suss?'

More bumps. These people were not at all quiet.

'Well, shit.'

'Just take it all.'

Catherine couldn't ignore the pain in her shoulders. She tried to distract herself by concentrating on which shoulder felt worse. The right felt like it was being split by a skewer, whereas the left felt more like the large area from her trapezium to her elbow was on fire.

'What, the clothes?'

'No fuckwit, just look for the phone. It's a grey one. She told me. Or a laptop or anything that might have it.'

There was a thump down the hall.

'What's that?' the female voice called out.

'Nothing.'

'Jesus.'

Catherine's arm gave way. She tried not to call out, but fell, looking downwards. Boris caught her, but her boot scraped his chest and he gave a surprised gasp.

They both heard the female voice above them. 'What's that?'

'Someone's here,' a male answered.

Ciara landed next to Boris soundlessly, hitting the ground before Boris had even put Catherine down.

Boris looked at Catherine. 'Run.'

They flew.

The three of them hurtled towards the street, the fog beginning to dissipate at the worst possible time. As they ran past the door, they heard it fling open. No one called out but Boris could hear feet on the steps following them. At the street, Catherine and Ciara veered left so Boris took a right. His feet pounded the pavement, looking madly for an alleyway. His ear bud was dropping out of his ear and his shoved it into his coat pocket, without breaking stride. He took the first side street and jumped a waist high concrete fence. He landed in a dirt patch in front of a Californian bungalow with no lights on inside. He had just missed a small rose bush. Small blessings.

He shoved a fist into his mouth and tried to breathe slowly through his nose, defying his lungs, which felt like fire. He counted to ten, getting to four before footsteps thumped past him, slowing as they went past the house. Boris saw a bearded face look in the garden of the next house along. He lay parallel to the fence. Holding his breath entirely. He heard a hand tap on the fence top and a grunt as the footsteps moved away.

He counted to ten. Then another ten. His lungs were about to burst. He took the fist out of his mouth and sucked in huge lungfuls of air. Blinking, sniffing, he let a tear of relief come. A second later he thought about Catherine and Ciara. Assuming all three breaker-inners were chasing them, that meant two had gone after his friends. He knew Ciara was fit, but Catherine's lungs would start to hurt after running a couple of blocks. Not that her fitness level was anything Boris could sneer about.

He was about to get up when the door in front of him opened. A Vietnamese woman of about sixty stood in front of him wearing a pink dressing gown; in her hand was a dog lead that was attached to a white pit bull, who seemed very interested in Boris. She blinked at him a few times, her mouth twitching.

'Shit, sorry. Gee.' Boris was up on his feet with his hands out before she could speak.

'You're a poor burglar.' The woman's Vietnamese accent was thick. He was grateful she was obviously quite strong. The dog wasn't getting closer despite straining at the leash.

'More a clumsy oaf looking for a place to rest.'

'Next time use the back garden. Better flowers, better smelling.' She pointed to where he had lain. 'That where the dog pisses every morning. Bad dreams down there.' She laughed and closed the door.

'Jesus.' Boris sat on the fence as he eased himself over. He smelled his sleeve. 'Jesus,' he said again., starting at a trot back to the car.

The sun was pushing the last of the fog away. He jogged a block before a police car rolled past and he realised he would be a lot less conspicuous if he walked. He could see the car, but no sign of Catherine or Ciara.

His phone chirped. He fished his earbud out of his pocket and came to an immediate stop. 'Catherine.'

'Are you clear?' She was very quiet.

'I am. You?'

'Yes and no. We thought we'd shaken them, but I can see them, so we were wrong. We're in Debney Park off Victoria Street. Currently hiding in a play equipment pirate boat. The cover's not great. Can you drive around?'

Boris quickened his step. 'Yep. I'll be a couple of minutes.'

'Boris. I see three of them now. Ciara says the woman is Harley. They all look tough.'

Boris opened his car door and looked at his phone to find where Debney Park was. 'Is she freaking out?' Boris turned on the ignition and put the car in drive.

Catherine replied in a sing-song voice. 'That's an affirmative. We have to avoid recognition as a priority. Okay, they're closing in. We may need a diversion.'

Boris drove, checking his phone for directions. It was just around the corner. The car started whining. 'Closing in.' he said. He hung up.

'If this bloody car doesn't die.'

Catherine held Ciara's hand as they peeped through the porthole of the SS *Adventure*. She ignored the fact that her knuckles may break – Ciara was gripping harder than she had gripped Silver's balcony. Catherine watched the three followers approach.

'Boris is coming.'

Ciara's mouth was twitching. 'What can he do?'

'Trust him.'

Catherine watched the three, getting a good look for the first time.

Harley was taller than she'd seemed on stage: dyed red hair, obviously athletic and more than beautiful. She had large eyes and full lips. Catherine registered the eyes first. Even if she didn't know Harley's reputation she would have watched herself around her. Some eyes seem very comfortable not caring about, well, anyone. Her default setting seemed to be haughty.

Ciara shivered next to her. Not because of the cold. Whoever Harley really was, she had a grip on people. Catherine decided she didn't like her one whit.

The two men look like brothers. Both tall, and muscular. One sported a beard and a bald head, the other a ponytail. They both wore leather jackets over hoodies, but without any visible gang markings. They were checking out the secondary playground, where a ship of a different name was searched with no prisoners found. Harley pointed to the park where she and Ciara hid.

Boris' car pulled up on the street.

Catherine checked for a back way out of the park. There was a row of fences, 100 metres from them. They might make it, but Ciara would be sprung. Catherine wondered what Boris could offer.

Boris got out and yelled at the top of his voice. 'Oi, Vince.'

'Oh Christ,' Catherine murmured.

'What?' Ciara asked in a voice so high she could almost be crying.

'He's doing Dodgy Kevin.'

Boris hobbled as quickly as he could to the trio. He kept his arm up in a huge wave and smiled a lopsided smile. He made his voice a high pitched whine, a good octave higher than his usual.

'Hi. Hey. Hi.'

The three looked at him askance. One of the blokes squared up, even though he was thirty metres away.

'You must be Vince. I'm Kevin.' Boris tapped his chest. 'I'm Boof's mate. He said I'd find you here. Did he text yas?'

'Piss off.' Ponytail gave a dismissive gesture. They turned back to the playground.

'Nah mate. Nah.' Boris just got louder and louder. 'Don't be like that. Boof said you were cool. Look man, I just really need a sting. Y'know?' Boris was within five metres now, the three turned back toward him. 'Which one of youse is Vince? Eh?'

Baldy pushed Boris away. 'Fuck off, brassy. No fucking Vince here.'

Boris fell back on his arse and yelped. Baldy and the woman were looking around as the light increased around them. 'Come on, man. You're not here for play group. Just gimme a sting and I'll leave ya. I've got thirty bucks right here, mate.'

Baldy moved. 'I'll give ya a fucking sting.'

Boris feinted as the blow came down, twisting to give the man a sharp one on the side of the head. The bald man looked perplexed. Boris hadn't hurt him, but he wasn't expecting a blow from a junkie. Boris amped the volume up a notch. 'C'mon dickhead. I'll smash all of youse.'

Three pairs of eyes went from him to the entire park. Boris hoped a flash of pink he saw in the background was an early-rising toddler. He found still more volume.

'I'll smash all of you.'

Baldy came in close, more graceful than Boris had expected, but he ducked the man's blow, which glanced off his cheek. Boris countered with a body jab that landed almost convincingly. Boris bellowed like an adenoidal banshee. A second later he saw the woman pull Baldy back and then the three of them ran. At the end of the park, a woman in pink stood with a stroller in front of her and her phone to her ear.

Boris watched them go. It was all clear in twenty seconds.

Then he heard the crying from the pirate ship.

Catherine walked out, holding Ciara, who seemed fit to faint.

'Are you right to walk?' Boris asked, his voice and stance back to normal.

'That was so silly. You are brave, but so stupid.' Ciara hit him in the chest while Catherine suppressed a smile.

'Yeah, you sound like my ex. It was all I could think of.'

'You did well, dear. One of these days you're going to write a full show for the fringe festival.' Catherine touched his face. 'That sore?' She showed him the blood on her finger.

'Just a little. He must have had a ring on.' Boris looked at the car. 'Let's get out of here before they come back or the cops come.'

The woman in pink was still on her phone and watching them closely. Boris gave her a broad smile and a wave as they got into the car.

'Ciara?' Boris asked as he let off the hand break.

'Yes?'

'Any good cafes around here? I believe Catherine owes me a hearty breakfast, right dear?'

Catherine gave him a slow blink that he didn't see, but knew was there anyway. 'I suppose, dear.'

Ciara groaned, leaning back on the seat. 'Personally, I think I'll just throw up.'

A quiet drive and a short walk later, they were at a café table with a round of coffees was in front of them. At Six Points Cafe in Moonee Ponds, the décor was cheerful and woody. The waiter had been efficient and it all felt about a thousand miles from being chased and hit by thugs. Catherine pointed out Boris smelled worse than usual after a chase. From the distance of a few seats, he quietly recounted the story of the dog and the fence line and was relegated to the foot of the table after that. Luckily the café was quiet so they could speak without whispering.

There were long silences as the three of them moved through various stages of emotion and adrenaline. Boris rubbed his face. Catherine rotated her shoulder.

'Catherine, your arm will hurt for a bit. I was able to hold on because I'm trained. The lactic acid in your arms must have made it difficult.'

'It did. How much longer did you have?'

'About five minutes until the acid gets too much.' She smiled and turned to Boris. 'Boris, you have,' Ciara smiled a little for the first time, 'played that clown before?'

Boris took a long sip of his latte. 'It came to me once when Catherine had to get away from a bad date quickly. Dodgy Kev is three things: loud, horrible and utterly familiar. He makes people go away quicker than saying you want to discuss Jesus.'

'He is effective.' Catherine toasted him with her coffee. 'Well. I call that a success.'

Ciara blinked. 'How?'

'We know that Harley is looking for things, Harley knows someone else is looking for things, and she doesn't know for certain it's you.'

'Doesn't she?' Boris countered. 'Ciara was hit last night, and the troupe is pretty small. If she assumes that whoever is on to her is in the performing troupe, who does that leave?'

'There are five more girls.' Ciara winced. 'Sorry, four. And Virginia.' Her forefinger traced the rim of her long black.

Catherine took out her small book. 'What are their names?'

'Megan, Lana, Rochelle and Jean.'

'And we'll get to them. I want to talk about what Harley was looking for.'

'I heard papers, phone and laptop. Also, remember she said she was looking for the dago bitch.' Ciara pointed to herself, grimly.

'Oh yes, I'm sorry she said that. But all the better they didn't find you.'

'I've heard it before.'

Boris and Catherine tried to think of something to say. There wasn't anything. Catherine moved back to business. 'So, they were looking for laptops, papers, phone. Why?'

Boris shrugged and looked to see if his breakfast was coming. 'Why would anyone steal that kind of thing? Identity theft?'

'Seems odd to me,' Catherine continued. 'Why be in a circus troupe, then kill someone, just to get a laptop? That doesn't make sense, unless you know something is on said piece of equipment.'

'So Harley knew a secret of Silver's or vice versa and Harley's trying to find proof of it. Or perhaps something about the death?'

'Well, Harley was the director, maybe something about that trick?'

Ciara shook her head. 'No, that trick was so small in comparison to other parts. It's more like nasty messages about either Silver or others.'

Boris paused, coffee halfway to his mouth. 'Why look for a phone at her house? Surely it would have been with her at the show?'

'I don't know, maybe she has two?'

Boris nodded. Catherine looked at the red mark on the left side of his face where "Kevin" had been hit. She wondered if they should get him some ice.

'There must be some messages that Harley doesn't want to get out. Maybe bullying, maybe worse.'

Catherine squeezed a serviette in her hand, idly. 'She's that bad?'

'She would break into a woman's apartment in the dead of night, just two days after she dies in front of her.'

'Yes, well.' Boris began, 'but we don't really have a leg to stand on there, do we?'

The food arrived. Boris's plate was all the colours of a future coronary. Catherine's eggs seemed decadent compared to Ciara's fruit platter.

'Could I get a little ice, mate?' Boris asked the waiter. He gestured to his face. 'Cut myself shaving.'

The waiter smiled.

Catherine shook her head. 'You're a better actor than a liar.'

'I like to think I have a roguish charm.'

'You have hollandaise in your beard, Han Solo.'

Boris scrambled with the paper serviettes.

Ciara drained her coffee and signalled the waiter, *same again, all round.* Catherine liked that she didn't ask. After the morning she'd had, she was considering champagne.

'The other performers in the show. Who's the best to start with?'

Ciara chewed a piece of pear and thought about it. 'Jean. Jean is the one we all like, she's the easiest to be with. Harley didn't bully Jean. It would seem impossible.'

'Is she tough?'

'No, she's just very, very herself. You know those people.'

Catherine looked at Boris for a fraction of a second.

'Yeah, I do. Okay, I'll start there.' The hollandaise was delicious and she felt like perhaps they were getting somewhere. 'Tell me more about the friendship between Silver and Harley. I'm trying to get a sense of what she's worried about.'

'They were hot and cold. Harley was so good at mind games. Silver went along with it because that made life easier for you in the troupe. Like I told, Harley was the centre of the troupe, like the sun. The closer you were, the warmer it got.'

And the opposite too, Catherine surmised. 'Were they ever intimate?'

'No. Harley only likes boys. Only big boys too. But that wouldn't be what they were looking for even if they had fucked. It's circus. No one gives a shit about sex.'

Boris smiled at that. 'Speaking of boys, did you recognise the fellows Harley was with?'

'No. I haven't seen them before. They look like bikers, no?'

'Yeah, but the one who hit me moved pretty easily. They weren't circus people?'

'They could be. I didn't recognise them, but I don't know all the circus men. Our troupe was set up as all women. It seems old fashioned now. Harley wanted to end that.'

'She wanted men?'

'Non binary, intersex. She says gender is bullshit.'

The waiter returned with the coffees and some ice wrapped in a tea towel. Boris pressed it to the side of his face.

There was a few seconds of silence, then groaning, almost sub-audibly. Catherine looked at Ciara as the woman snorted into her wrist. 'What?'

Ciara kept laughing, Catherine found herself laughing too.

'I'm sorry. I'm thinking of Boris doing that clown again. I shouldn't laugh.' She took a breath and sipped her coffee. 'Boris, I had a sense about you yesterday. That you were someone who was good at helping people. I was right, I think.'

Boris blushed pink and murmured something that tried to be self-effacing, but was mostly growling. He righted himself with coffee. Ciara kept laughing and Catherine, likely a touch delirious after the morning, joined in.

'Back to the troupe, though. What about bullying?' Boris countered. 'Is that so frowned upon? I don't know much about circus, but I knew some really mean actors.'

Ciara nodded. 'Yes, that is true too. One person's monster is another's difficult genius. The better you are for the show, the more you can get away with.'

Catherine sawed at some toast. Even with all this coffee a nap was looking good. 'Did you see anything in the papers you were looking through? Aside from spooking Harley, and this could be a coffee comedown, but maybe we didn't achieve as much as I'd hoped.'

'You said it was a success?' Boris sounded wounded.

'Well, you got hit, I strained my shoulders and the whole thing was my idea, so I had to give it a positive spin. Pessimists will only end up with smug drinking problems.'

'You can drink, ah, smug tonight.' Ciara chirped. 'I think Harley is on to me, but that wasn't the only reason I didn't want her to find us at the playground.'

Catherine and Boris both leaned in.

'Yes?'

Ciara pulled something out of her pocket. Sleek, grey, rectangular and small.

A grey Nokia lay on the table in front of them. 'I found it near the table. I didn't want to say until I knew we were safe.'

5

I'm all for living in the now, but can I also live in the now while not freezing?
~Boris Shakhovskoy

'That was quite the mic drop. Don't you think?'

With Ciara having gone to work at the café, Catherine decided she, too, should put in a few hours at the grindstone that was her studio. It was raining outside and the studio's high windows gave the impression that she was inside an elaborate goldfish bowl. Boris, who didn't start his shift for another two hours, was half napping on the green Persian couch Catherine kept for clients to sit on. As she had no clients today, and since he had showered and got into some spare clothes, Catherine had allowed it.

'Yeah, she's a performer.' He drawled, eye half closed.

'That's my worry.'

Boris said nothing, but picked up the notepad that held all the information they had on the phone Ciara had found. The phone itself had been scanned for fingerprints and bagged for future reference. There was one visible notification. From a contact: "D"

Everything you need, and ever could need, is in the ga.

Catherine spoke as she concentrated on the hat in her hands. 'My money's still on some kind of herb.'

'Garnish?'

'You use herbs as garnish, or in garnish, garnish isn't itself a herb.'

Boris ignored this. 'My money's on garage. I don't see why a herb leads to murder, no matter how good the tarragon is.'

'Tarragon?' Catherine almost dropped her ribbon. 'I swore you only knew one herb, which you didn't use for cooking.'

Lying down and shrugging is difficult for most people, Boris managed it easily. 'I'm growing older. You can't be Cheech and Chong forever.'

'They seem to be doing a good job.'

'Point. See how valuable herbs can be, they're still supple in their twilight years.' Boris got up, grunting as if to make a point.

'Don't tell me you're sore. You weren't hanging from a balcony for a quarter of an hour.'

'Neither were you.'

Catherine rolled her eyes. 'How many people outside of primary school age hung from their arms for longer than me today? Ciara, a few gymnasts and a clumsy tree surgeon. That's my hit prediction. I have earned this whinging time.'

'Have you called Neal?'

She didn't look at him. 'I texted.'

'Oh, bad move.'

'Why?'

Boris lazily moved his back and felt a crack that made no sound. 'He'll see how long it's been since you last texted him. You know he gets annoyed when you only go to him when he's useful.'

Catherine finished her twirls and looked at Boris for the first time in the conversation. 'Oh please, he has the patience of a saint. Plus, in three months will be a father for the first time. Plus I texted him last week.'

'Really?'

'I wondered if I could borrow June's jewellery for a fashion event.'

'So technically?'

'I needed something.' Catherine sniffed. 'I hang my head in shame. I am a terrible friend and a worse sister.'

Boris looked across the room at the single photo of Catherine's family. 'I wasn't bringing that up, and you're lovely to me. If your sister ever wants to whinge I'll defend you to the hilt.'

Catherine stood and arranged her tools on the side desk. 'Only because you get hit in the head for me periodically.'

Boris stood, touching the cut. 'True. But I'm good at that. Sure I could make more money as a body man to a mob boss, but I doubt the repartee would be the same.'

'Body man?'

He smiled. 'Would you prefer hired goon?'

'Cherished and revered friend.'

He embraced her. Catherine was saved from affectionately noticing his armpit smell by the sound of her phone ringing.

'Neal, my favourite two thirds of a parent.'

'And enjoying my last days of freedom I can tell you. I was asleep when you texted. I stayed up last night watching Canada versus Bangladesh in women's cricket.'

'How modern of you!'

'Ah, my dear Catherine, I wasn't virtue signalling. I'll watch any cricket played by someone better than me. Which would include most women, I assure you. I've been a fan of Jahanara Alam for years.'

Catherine grinned at the muted warble of her friend's laughter.

'The child is a girl, no?'

'Correct. Bad luck in my culture, but bad luck to my culture for its short-sightedness!' Catherine could imagine the gestures that would accompany such a phrase.

'You're a delight, Nealamber Singh.'

'Now, were you calling to discuss the leg spin of Alana King??'

Catherine studiously didn't meet Boris' amused gaze. 'Ah, not today. I was wondering if I could use your brains to solve a mystery.'

'A robbery?'

'A death, and I'm not sure what else.'

'Ahh.' The laughter came again, though with a hint of a regretful overtone. 'And once again your respect for Victoria's finest is evident.'

'It's not about respect for them, it's about concern for a friend. This time yesterday I was sure this was just an accident. Now I know that something unsavoury is happening and I want to understand. I know, I'm a control freak.'

There was a silence. For some reason. Catherine imagined him rearranging his desk for better organisation as he considered her request. 'Okay, what do you need from me? June is nesting and I could use the distraction from listening to her alphabetise the pantry again.'

'It's a phone hack for now. I'll pop it over to you.'

'I'll get the tools out and pop the kettle on.'

As she hung up, Boris raised an eyebrow from the article he was pretending to read on her iPad. 'He's in. Didn't even make a thing of it. He's enjoying the last months of being a non-parent.'

'You mean having something needy that stops him sleeping enough?' Boris stifled a yawn.

'Oh hush, dear.'

It stopped raining just as Catherine fired up her Vespa and waved to Boris, who was going home seeking a nap or more caffeine before work. A few chilly minutes later and she was walking up the path towards Neal's cosy East Brunswick abode. She was greeted by June, who looked equally resplendent and whale-like.

'My dear.' June took Catherine's face in her palm.

'You look beautiful!' Catherine beamed. 'How are you feeling?'

'Like a tired walrus. But a happy one. Nealamber is being his usual gentlemanly self, even when he stays up late he arrives at my bed with tea before I've so much as blinked. I think he needs this.' She patted her belly, looking up the hallway as Neal came down it in a stiff white-collared shirt covered by a rich red woollen cardigan. 'When a man is so hell-bent on being middle aged, he should at least have a child to talk about at parties.'

Catherine made a noise like a Lego set under pressure as Neal joined them.

'Did she make comment about my style?' He beamed. 'What is it about women that find something charming until they become pregnant?'

'Hormones dear, they are a great awakener,' June scoffed, huffing slightly.

Catherine cut between them. 'I think it's the feeling of having actually hitched one's wagon. Permanence is not a sexy look.'

'I completely disagree, Catherine.' Neal gazed at his wife with a look that gave Catherine a moment of difficult joy. Find a lover who looks at you the way Neal looks at June. It was definitely on her to do list.

His eyes snapped back to Catherine. 'Now, what's the job?'

Catherine brought the phone out of her pocket. 'Just seeing what you can do with this.'

She followed Neal and June back up the hallway. Their living room was the highlight of their house, airy and light, with the waft of their beautiful and expansive garden mingling with the air even in this stark season. Every time Catherine walked into to it, she had a sense of a magician's reveal. Their artwork was beautiful, their taste muted and elegant.

Today though, with so much on her mind Catherine hardly looked at the decor before she followed Neal out of the backdoor, casting an eye back to see June collapse on their spacious red couch. A few steps through the cool and they came to Neal's furnished – and heated – working space. A two-room studio where he worked most days before returning to home and hearth. Catherine had been told – in confidence – that he still sometimes complained of the commute.

Catherine started giving him the story of the past two days as Boris took in the room. Neal's usual stock–in-trade of school music software took up a great deal of the office's western side, as did a large picture of Dolly Parton. He and Catherine moved beyond this to the eastern partition where Neal's favourite toys were in place. An array of pliers, electronics and computer boxes lined his benches. The only nod that wasn't to his work was an old cricket ball nestled amongst the soldering irons and electronic chip boards.

Neal shook himself, like an athlete before the race. 'The phone itself. Is it the deceased's?'

She passed it to him. 'It was found at the deceased's house. I'm still on the fence about the death being suspicious.' She watched Neal's cursory first inspection. 'Though Boris has a bruise. So I believe something's up.'

'Not,' he looked up meaningfully, 'self-inflicted, this time?'

'No. He took a punch for a couple of dames.'

Neal smiled as he started up a pale laptop. 'Violence is never the answer, yet never goes away. Blessed is the man who protects women.'

'That's an almost acceptable level of sexism there, Neal.'

'I'm not the one who let a fella take a punch for me, Catherine,' he retorted. She noted, both his almost invisible wink and his dropping of the usual 'My dear.' And was annoyed by his quickness.

Neal wasn't staying on the topic, though. He scanned the screen. 'Everything you need, and ever could need, is in the ga.' He looked at Catherine. 'The deceased was an Indian lady?'

'No. I only saw her for a distance, but I'm sure she was Anglo. Why?'

'My thought was the Ganges. Which betrays the birthplace of my father.'

'Ganges.' Catherine touched an eyebrow. 'Silver was a circus performer, and something of a hippy even in that world. It could be the Ganges. You'll note though that it's sent by someone only known as "D". Also it would make sense that it's something, forgive me, hippy. All you'll ever need.'

'You don't believe in a singular balm that can solve your problems?'

'I like gin and tonic and lime, and a glass. That's four things.'

'And more than one of them.'

'Let's be civil Neal, it's cold outside.'

Neal beamed beatifically. 'Have you only brought me this? You usually bring me prints with such a job.'

Catherine brought out some cling wrap in a zip lock bag. 'I did the initial work myself.'

'So I won't be looking up both you and Boris again?'

'Possibly only one of us.'

'Let's see what we can find.' He turned back to his computer and plugged the phone in with an extension.

The words came up quickly: Cannot access device. Contact scheme administrator.

Catherine looked at Neal. 'Is that bad?'

'No.' He hit some keys and clicked through several screens showing either java language or some other form of Bahasa technologica. After six screens he hummed.

Three words were onscreen: orca 19>5//

Catherine blinked as she stared. 'What does that mean?'

'Something serious, I'm afraid. It means I don't know. I haven't seen this code before.'

'And that means?'

Neal kept typing meditatively. 'That it could take me a day or a month. The answer will not be quick. I'm sorry Catherine.'

She chewed her mouth, suddenly tired. 'Ah no problem. That means I'll do it the old fashioned way. Do you even have time?'

'In between overs tonight, I'll give it my full attention. Our cause is righteous is it not?'

'Always, Neal. You're the best.'

He smiled ruefully as he settled into battle with the machine. 'I love a challenge. No one brings me better challenges than you.'

Catherine gestured towards the house. 'I suspect that will change in coming months.'

An hour later, Catherine was feeling challenged herself.

'It's just really got to me today.' Virginia, slumped back on the couch, spilled just a sip of champagne onto one of Catherine purple and mustard cushions, her big personality having pushed itself through Catherine's door a few minutes earlier.

Catherine, with her own champagne to guide her good mood, nodded. 'It's natural, of course. There's no rule book for grief.'

'I appreciate how good you're being. I just want to know how this could happen.'

'Has there been any indication of how long the coroner's report will take?'

'The police said they're pushing to make it quick due to the public nature of the death. Oh, there's just trauma everywhere.'

Virginia went into small convulsions. Catherine patted her shoulder, and while convention said a hug was needed, the woman had a carnivorous air that Catherine didn't want to feed. Even if the woman did bring over a bottle of Mumm at 3.40pm on a Thursday.

Virginia took her hand and squeezed hard. Then let go, possibly too distraught to remain lecherous.

'Now I'm dealing with her family.' Her voice caught. 'It's so unfair. I,' she pointed to her chest, 'had been her family for three years. Those stuck up pricks have hardly spoken to her in all that time.'

Catherine sat up. 'Who are they?'

Virginia looked out the window at the grey air covered in grey clouds, gesticulating disgust. 'Big house in Lakes Entrance. Sporty brothers. Father's in some kind of metal business.'

'You know them?'

'He spoke to me last night. It's why I'm here.' She moved a fraction closer.

Catherine leaned back. She hated men not getting a hint; in a woman, it was just disappointing. 'He wants a hat for his grieving?'

'He's like me. He wants to know what happened. He's willing to pay you for a three month examination of her life. Just so he knows why she died.'

'He's heard of me?'

'No. I told him about the kidnapping case. And about the business in Ocean Grove last summer.'

Catherine's shoulders tensed. 'How did you know about that?'

'You told me about it at the Night Cat two months ago. You remember that night after the show in town?'

Catherine bumped the couch twice. 'Ah yes, that night. I remember at least two quarters of that night.'

Virginia took an unladylike gulp of champagne and Catherine felt compelled to applaud. 'I gave him your number. His name is Anthony. He's horrible.'

'Thanks a million.' Catherine looked for Minty, in need of feline consolation.

'But he's rich.'

Catherine felt her face knit. 'Why do people always think that makes it okay to be horrible?'

'Because most of us aren't.'

Catherine watched a plane move across the sky, through her window and above Fawkner simultaneously. 'Horrible? I'm not so sure.'

'I mean rich, darling. Another?' She closed in with the bottle.

'Oh.' Catherine held out her glass. Always an upside to every moment.

As much as he tried to love every season, which was Catherine's influence, Boris struggled with this time of year. Melbourne, early July. When every day made you remember just how long something unpleasant, and cold, could go on for. He failed to see the romance, at least sober. At this moment, working up to a shift, having been up early, being hit and deciding not to have a nap earlier, he felt decidedly unromantic. Winter was suffering and dull and forever and this was Samsara in its purest form and woe betide the bastard who pushed dharma on him anytime soon.

He regretted the thought as he saw someone in the distance whom he had deceived very recently. The transition from sulking to fear can quickly make a person miss merely sulking.

A short but intimidating woman with a shock of dyed red hair was moving towards him in a way that made Boris think that coincidences didn't happen. Harley sashayed over Sydney Road like she owned it.

Before she crossed his path, Boris walked through the door of the Palace, with five minutes until his shift started. He continued through to the kitchen. After greeting the locals and the staff he looked at the knives on the magnetic plate above the galley. He was suddenly, painfully aware that he was good in the moment, but terrible in an actual fight. If he escalated to knives, he would end up stabbed. He knew it as a fact.

'Okay, Boris?' Jamie, the chef, seemed concerned as he pulled a deep fryer basket of chips out of the oil. 'You look spooked.'

'Just saw a woman I didn't want to see again.'

Jamie nodded knowingly. 'Been there, man. Did you only see her the once?'

'Um, yeah.'

'Just pretend you're someone else. Man, I do it all the time.'

The chef returned to plating up the parmas. Jamie was tall, lean and somehow not pale in July. Boris was sure that most women saw him and Jamie as not so much different types, but different species. While he wasn't so shallow as to say good looks got everything, he strongly identified as someone not spunky enough to lie to anyone. Plus, the idea of pretending to be someone else sounded awful.

With these thoughts in mind, he moved through the function room, mostly to avoid the chill of the garden corridor. Maybe she hadn't come into the Palace. Maybe she wasn't here for him. Maybe she was here for Jamie.

In the front bar, Boris took up position behind the taps, and there she was. Perched on a bar stool in the middle of the room. She flicked through a street press magazine, but she was looking straight at him. Boris kept his face neutral and took an order for a pint.

He looked around the bar. The early after-work crowd was slow, as it usually was this time of year. Boris would have far too much time to not be busy unless people came to the counter quickly. Then again, why delay the inevitable? If the gig was up, so be it.

After fifteen minutes, she came to the bar. Boris was suddenly aware of how damp his armpits were.

'What'll you have?'

'Information.' She was bright and her voice had a lift that didn't belong in winter.

'You get that at the kitchen counter.'

'Your face all right?' Her voice was flat now. As was her stare. Boris was aware of people noticing the interaction.

He kept it neutral. 'Training injury.'

'What do you play?'

Boris blinked. 'Croquet.' He gave a humourless smile. 'Some people have a hell of a swing.'

'Don't they? You haven't seen anything, and I can find you anytime.' She kept up the hard stare.

'Drink?' He pointed to a man behind her. 'He wants one.'

'I don't drink.'

'Cool.' He moved to the tall local. 'Glass of cab sav, Stevie?'

Harley stood in front of the bespectacled man. 'I'll be taking what you took from me.' She tapped the bar twice and moved away.

Boris let out a breath very slowly. His mouth tasted like a hangover.

Stevie stepped to the bar with a raised eyebrow and an open mouth. 'What the hell did you take from her?'

Boris shrugged. 'Her cheery disposition.'

Two hours later, Catherine walked into the Palace.

As she slid into her usual stool, she took in the twinkle of the candles and the murmur of the locals. As she rubbed the small amount of rain that had wet her hair in the 321 metre walk to the pub, Boris mixed her a drink. She blinked back the rain and the fatigue that had, almost, kept her home.

'I note you've made me a double. I'm not sure I need it.'

He grinned, and looked ten years older than usual. 'Well maybe I do and I'm drinking by osmosis.' He set it down and picked up her credit card.

'Wait.' She blinked. 'Do you have a girlfriend I've forgotten about who's dumped you? I can't remember what part of the cycle we're in.'

'Cute.' He tossed the card back like a ninja star. 'Ask Stevie.'

'Wait, I have news.'

'I've run out of Coburg Lager, give me a minute.'

Stevie sidled up. Catherine took a moment to welcome this local of indomitable cheer and indestructible liver.

'Stevie, what is Boris talking about?'

Stevie pointed to the door Boris had just disappeared into. 'I officially have no idea who that man is.'

'Talk to me.'

He took off his glasses. 'Well. I know you love him almost as much as I do. But we both know that any woman he speaks to has a certain power over him.'

'A gift he gives freely, and without anyone wanting it.'

'True.' Glasses back in place, Stevie rolled a smoke as he spoke. 'Well. I came to the bar and he's talking, nah, he's being spat bile at by a she-monster of well, epic curves. Even I noticed.'

'Who is she?'

Stevie's chin dropped 15 degrees to better eyeball Catherine. 'Your height, amazing eyes, dyed red hair. I don't know who she is, but she hates your boy. And, while she was throwing down, Mr Wimpy over there just stayed tough and played her like he was James Dean.' He put the smoke between his lips and raised both arms in defeat. 'I have no idea who he is.' With that, Stevie sauntered down to the beer garden, where he would smoke in a thin shirt in artic breezes and never complain.

Boris walked back, served a pint and went to Catherine. 'Have you worked it out?'

Catherine, who hadn't stopped looking at Boris like he was some kind of strange plant, leaned forward. 'Stevie says a beautiful redhead was threatening you and you played it cool as the proverbial. I'm guessing Harley came in for a drink?'

'She doesn't drink.'

Catherine inhaled with a grin. 'Hmm.'

'She's pretty confident she's going to get what I took from her.'

'You should send word to dodgy Kevin. Boris, Stevie said you played it cool. I'm amazed.'

'Because I'm usually so bad when a woman speaks to me?'

'Unless they're asking for a drink, yes, you are a special kind of hopeless.'

Boris rubbed his face. 'Yes, but I'm usually terrified of disappointing people and them hating me, I'm already there with Harley.'

'Well, you're always good in the pinch.' Catherine took a long sip. 'It's your defining feature.'

'Catherine,' Boris spoke quietly. 'We're in the pinch. That's why I could play it cool. She's business. She's pretty fearless, and she's coming for me.'

'Yep. And you'll match her. And you'll find out what she wants and that will lead us to what happened.' Catherine held his gaze. 'This isn't our usual speed, but it's where we always end up. You'll be fine.'

'I wish I had your confidence.'

'Or we walk. You call in sick and I'll get you a flight to somewhere warm in the next hour. You're worth it. There's always options.'

He smiled. 'Would you come?'

'Can't yet, too curious.'

'Then I'll hang around too. Thanks for offering though. France would be lovely this time of year.'

'I was thinking Balina. I make hats for a living, dude.'

Boris smiled and moved off to serve other patrons while Catherine ran the numbers. Harley obviously wasn't a subtle player. If she was behind hitting Ciara last night and then threatening Boris, that put her on the hot and impulsive end of the cold and calculating spectrum. That could be exploited.

Impulsive. The word stayed with her. So was she. Catherine imbibed a little juniper goodness to soften the self-thought and accurate blow. She'd started the day doing the same thing as Harley, breaking into Silver's house. The only difference was that Harley knew what she was looking for. It wasn't a game.

Catherine watched Boris move, fixated on his cut face. More than once she had wondered how it would feel if he died working for her.

Her glass was empty. Some thoughts do that.

Catherine watched Boris laugh with Stevie while pouring wine. If she could stop hearing the crack of Silver's neck for just a few minutes, maybe she could call this investigation off. A week in Darwin with Boris could be good for both of them.

Boris caught her eye. She thought of Ciara.

If she let it go, he wouldn't, even if she did send him to France. He would try to do it himself. Of course he would.

She signalled for another drink.

Hours later, they walked back to Catherine's apartment. Boris didn't say much, seemed to be watching a tennis match that Catherine couldn't see.

'You're vigilant.' Catherine looked around, mirroring his swivelling neck over the past few hundred metres.

'A bit jumpy. Those blokes this morning were handy.'

'Fair. You're handy too.'

'You've pumped up my tyres enough for one night.' Boris took a sip of his drink. The weather had calmed but the air was still and cold. 'No one usually knows that until I'm in the fight already. I've always hated a build-up.'

'Yeah. You take no pleasure in the drama.'

'I just never got it. If someone needs to fight, just get it out of the way. I hate the pretence of the "I'm coming to get you" that makes you feel like,' he looked both ways up the road. 'well, this.'

'It's your usual issue, Boris.'

'What? B.O.?'

Catherine laughed, enjoying Boris smiling a little too. 'No, dear. It's power.'

'That I don't have it?'

She touched his face. 'No one has it, dear. It's just that you don't want it.'

He grinned a little, his breath fogging in the cold. 'Night.'

'You won't come in?'

'We started today at five in the morning. I'm exhausted. And I need a shower. That B.O. gag was only half a joke.'

Catherine smiled. He was right.

He turned up the rail line towards his house.

6

Most people quite like themselves, they just want a slightly different body and to be less interested in what they're usually doing at eleven at night.
~Catherine Kint

Boris saw no one else until he was past Moreland Road. He had almost relaxed and was enjoying watching his breath condense in the air when he saw movement in his peripheral vision.

Male, he was eighty per cent sure. Red jacket, dark jeans. Shorter than him. Possibly stumbling. The figure was illuminated by the yellow light of the streetlamp outside Moreland Station. Boris slowed. Looked up a side street as a way out. It was dimly lit, deserted, and further from home if it did come to a chase.

The figure was indeed stumbling. But after the Dodgy Kevin routine, he was ready to have his con played back. Boris stayed completely still. Why pretend it wasn't happening? It either was or it wasn't, pretending would change nothing. The figure lumbered on. Definitely male, Caucasian. Boris blinked, wishing he'd kept it to two drinks after work.

It definitely wasn't either of the blokes from the park. This man was shorter and wearing a fur hat that would seem hipster in any other month of the year. Boris stood completely still. Arms against his sides. He felt a chill as his face sweated against the air. He flexed his fingers. The man crossed the road diagonally, moving away from him. Boris turned to watch him.

Once the stranger hit the pathway, he turned and looked straight at Boris. The lope that had carried him across the street disappeared. He stood straight. Almost Boris's height. Shoulders back.

Boris felt the blood drain from his face. His throat was dry. His ears strained to hear the footsteps of the coming attack. No sound came. Then from a long way away, the hoot of a train joined the sound of his pulse, which was surely audible right down the Upfield line.

Red jacket called out. 'Can I help you friend?' The voice was light, but had a gravelly undertone. The vapour of his breath in the cold air gave the potential menace another element.

'No,' Boris's voice was almost a whisper. 'Not looking for help.'

There was a pause. Boris thought he heard footsteps, but it was a bat flying just three metres overhead. He swallowed. 'Are you looking for me?'

The man softened, his shoulders came down. 'No.' He exhaled heavily. 'I have no idea who you are mate, and I don't want to.'

More sweat beaded on Boris' neck. 'Right.' He held up a hand. 'Sorry, mate.' He stepped back and leaned against the concrete fence behind him. 'Long day.'

'Gotta watch that stuff mate, that tough guy act is a self-fulfilling prophecy.'

Boris let out a rush of breath that was pain disguised as a laugh. The man in the red jacket walked slowly past him. The lope was back, but instead of a tough-acting drunk he suddenly just seemed like a tipsy hippy. A ray of light caught his face as he passed: whiskered, lined. The lines a smile gives you rather than a scowl. He caught Boris' eye. Didn't smile then, but no malice.

This was no man to be afraid of. Neither was Boris, yet they were both ready. Boris watched him move away. In a minute he was gone. Boris looked at the sky. By his reckoning, he'd had five hours sleep in the last forty.

'Not an excuse, but a reason.'

He didn't look over his shoulder once the rest of the way home. Though he kept listening for footsteps.

Catherine had risen early, and blinked for a long time, staring out the window. When she looked at the grey clouds, when she felt the warmth of the coffee in her hand, when she saw the light change. She didn't hear the sound of a neck cracking as she stretched. She was still trying to notice every part of life, because Silver couldn't.

She was aware of where she had hurt her shoulder. The pain was not strident, but very, very present. She tried several different ways of moving it to soothe it, before giving up. Time wounds all heels. And it was only a small distraction from the gloomy nature of life.

When she touched the cat she wasn't part of a world where women were hit in the head on the very street she lived on. And where she put her best friend in danger because she needed to find things out.

After a time, she decided that concentrating on blinking and seeing should be part of everyone's morning practice. Time wasted is rarely *wasted*.

Finding things out was never achieved by wasting time.

First thing on her list – Silver's medical man in Sunshine. Anderson-or-Henderson-or-something-English, according to Ciara. After some false starts – GPs called Anderson, a vet called Henderson – Catherine found a likely candidate. A bespectacled fellow stared back at her from his online advert, looking concerned and competent. A replica skeleton a few metres behind him wore the grin that all bodies take with them long after their flesh is gone. In Catherine's opinion, skulls were the best indication that when it's all over we're still smiling.

She called the number on the ad.

'Active Energy Medical, this is Jordan, how can I help you?'

'Is this Jordan Harmison?'

'Yes, Doctor Jordan Harmison. Physio, chiro, and Eastern medicine.' His voice was even, but Catherine always had a small smile for people who needed to tell strangers what their qualifications were.

'Doctor, I'm Catherine. I'm having some trouble with energy and I was wondering if you had any time today.'

'What kind of energy issues?'

The lie came easily enough. 'Sometimes I'm tired even if I've had enough sleep.'

'Do you drink too much?'

Catherine shuddered, as if a goose was pouring gin on her grave. 'I wouldn't say that. But I would like to explore any option that works. I've been told you can work wonders. Do you have any time today?'

There was a pause. Catherine wondered if something she had said put him off. Then he came back, confident as before. 'I have a 9.45 today, as it happens. Does that work for you, ah, Catherine?' He had remembered her name too quickly. Attention to detail could sound creepy in a man sometimes.

Catherine's clock said 9am.

'Yes I can do that. See you then.'

'Ah, yes you will, Catherine.' She imagined him looking at the skeleton as he said it.

She put down her phone and exhaled. Eastern medicine, so far as she knew, took a more holistic approach to treating ailments than its western counterparts. She wondered if that was what was putting her off. There was something new age about it and about him. And she had hated new age for most of her life; even more so in recent years. If there was a wheatsheaf, a tarot card or even a hieroglyph she would abandon this whole thing very, very quickly.

She needn't have worried. While she Vespa'd over to Sunshine, she had imagined any number of horrendous shrines to well-being in Dr Harmison's studio, with at least two statues collected during his time studying on the subcontinent. She was even awaiting the quiet, wet whir of an ornate water fountain.

The carpark was sprawling, grungy, and about as far from a Zen garden as you could get. To get to Harmison's studio she had to walk through a cavernous gymnasium that managed to not be the arctic temperature inflicted on every other place in Melbourne. Catherine had already read the dozen annual articles about how the European winters weren't as harsh as Melbourne's, as they actually knew how to insulate. The articles came out every year, and never seemed to lose relevance.

Cold light filtered into the gym through high windows that had once lit a factory floor. Untouched bench presses lined one wall, with a dozen stair-masters on the opposite end. In the middle lay a dormant boxing ring, on one side of which a trainer coaxed a small man with strands of long hair combed over his balding pate through a series of focused exercises with a levered weight. His white singlet, of a fashion so far gone that even irony hadn't brought it back, was bulging slightly with each flex.

The trainer caught her eye and pointed disinterestedly toward the back of the building, as if expecting her. A motivational poster on the side wall showed a faded pineapple giving a thumbs up. Perhaps it was supposed to be inspiring, but to Catherine, it looked like an emoji had sneezed.

She caught the eye of a tall man on the other side of the building. Not a trainer, but in dark pants and an ironed shirt.

The man waved.

'Dr Harmison?'

'Just Jordan is fine. I assume you're Catherine?'

'Yes.'

'I say the doctor thing once, so people know, because some clients like to know I didn't just do "Bone Cracking for Dummies" as an online course. That's all.'

'Oh.' Catherine reassessed the man. 'Okay.'

He spoke as he walked. 'It's pretentious, I know, but people find it reassuring.' They moved beyond a dark brown curtain to two rooms. One was an office, the other held a massage table. Jordan gestured to the office.

'So how can I help?' He sat easily on his side of the neat desk. Catherine wondered when she had last misread someone so badly over the phone.

'I've been having some issues with energy. And a friend of mine said you had helped her. She's in a circus troupe.'

'Oh. Mia?'

'I know her as Silver.'

'I see. She did mention she performed under a different name. I had her booked in for an appointment. She didn't show. I hope she's okay.'

Catherine shrugged. 'I haven't spoken to her for a bit.'

Catherine couldn't read his expression, so she let the silence play out. She didn't know what else to do.

Jordan cleared his throat. 'Well, with Mia I was just exploring how to stop some blockages in chi that were occurring through her liver and pancreas. Are you in the circus too?'

'No. I've been around it a bit, but no.'

'Athlete?'

'I'm a milliner who enjoys drinking gin.'

'Right. I suspect we'll have to help your liver too, then.' He paused. 'Would you like to stop drinking gin?'

There was no accusation; it was like he was asking if she wanted cracked pepper on a meal. 'No.'

'You're sure?'

Catherine gave it 15 seconds' thought. Without gin she would have more money, sleep better, likely get along better with her mother. 'I'm positive. I'm good with the gin. That's not why I'm here.'

'Fine. Some people, well, what did Shakespeare say? Liquor is a good servant but a poor master.'

'I like my vices. I'm just tired.'

'Any pains?'

'Ah, my right shoulder hurts a bit. I had an accident yesterday, had to hang on to something for longer than I wanted to.'

'All right, can you raise your arm to the side? As high as it will go before it hurts.'

She moved it; stiff, but not sore.

'That's good, now I'm just going to put some resistance on it.' He pushed lightly against her arm and Catherine made an undignified sound.

'Right, there's the issue, I think. Can I look at the other arm as a reference point?'

She raised her left arm and even with the resistance it wasn't painful. She moved through a further series of movements at his guidance. He watched her muscles and movements with quiet attention.

Catherine thought of her body as a magical machine that was good at making hats and dancing. She was aware suddenly of the fragility and complexity of it. She decided to do some more reading on muscles as soon as she was able, just for the understanding. Just for the wonder.

'Okay, it's likely a strain rather than a tear. Let's get you on the table. I'll leave you to undress to your waist and lie down.' He gave no hint of anything but detached professionalism, so after he left, Catherine did exactly that. A minute later he returned and began some light effleurage, stroking her muscles in circular motions. Catherine was reminded how long it had been since her last massage and promised herself to do this more regularly.

After the past few days, this seemed the best part of investigation.

Whatever can't be investigated while being massaged was now officially outside her remit. After a while, Jordan became more targeted.

'I'm going take a closer look at your shoulder.'

He started some exploratory touching. All was well until he moved a finger into an area just left of her shoulder blade and she nearly jumped off the table. She made another sound that was both unfamiliar to her, and loud.

'Right, sorry, I won't touch there again.'

She felt she should respond. 'Ow.' She nodded gratefully into the table.

He was still massaging, but had taken a step back, which she appreciated. 'Yep, sorry. That's quite tender. This movement should get the blood flowing into the damaged area without touching it directly.'

'It's okay. I knew it was sore, but,' Catherine tried to think of a word, but all the languages she spoke failed her, 'ow.'

"Believe it or not, that's actually good news. You've strained your teres minor but I don't think you've torn it.'

'I felt torn just then.'

'It felt bruised, torn is worse.' His tone was gentle, but she believed him.

'Okay.'

'I'll put a compress on it and give you some needlework for your energy.'

'Oh, acupuncture?'

'Yes. It's a big part of my practice. Is, that okay?'

'Sure, had it before. In fact, the last time I had it was in Hong Kong a few years ago.' She yawned. 'When will you start putting them in?'

'I've started already.'

Catherine sniffed. It's always difficult to relax around a man who can stab you without you realising. Seriously. Men.

'How did you know Mia?'

Catherine was ready for this. 'We met on a tram and got chatting. I saw some of her circus work.'

'I've been meaning to watch.' His breathing didn't change at all. Catherine had been listening for it. 'She did silks, right?'

'You mean tissu?'

'Ah yeah, I think they're the same thing.'

Catherine kept her own voice light. Luckily she was facing down so she didn't have to concern herself with her facial expression. 'Has she been seeing you long?'

'About eight months. Athletes and performers can have regular flare ups. And she was having some trouble winding down. You can say the human body is able to do what they make it do, but there's probably reasons why most of us don't.'

'Do you have other athletes who come to you?' Catherine kept up the conversation as she started to feel sleep's pull.

'Yeah, lots of footy players, netball, athletics.'

'Any other circus people?'

'None, aside from Mia. Got a lot of martial artists, currently.'

Catherine felt a needle go into her skin, without pain, and gave herself over to experiencing without fear something that should be scary. 'Is there much difference between the footy players and the circus performers?'

'Less hamstring trouble in circus. Less sword swallowing in footy.'

'Hmp.'

'No, the nature of most injuries is we've asked a body to do something it shouldn't do, and it lets us know. Then it's about healing and finding a better way of doing it, either by strengthening the body or improving the technique.' He prodded her shoulder gently. 'How is that feeling now?'

'Hmm, much better already.'

'Oh good. Mia had a similar issue the other month, a silks accident she said.'

'Did she say what happened?'

'Just a twist that didn't go to plan.'

Catherine had to breathe for a few seconds after that one. 'Did you treat her the same way?'

'Yes, but I followed up with some herbs for energy and some others for sleep. I'm just going to give these a tweak.'

'Right. Should I have those too?'

There was a slight pause. 'Let's see how you respond to the needlework first. I think just this and a bit of rest and you'll be okay.' He stopped touching her. 'I'm going to leave those in for about ten minutes. I'll be in the other room, call out if anything gets painful.'

She heard his soft footfalls moving away.

She thought of Silver who had lain exactly here. Silver, who wanted herbs to feel more alive and now, presumably, felt nothing. Silver who had a twist that didn't go to plan.

On the other side of the room, her phone vibrated. She exhaled. No one ever got a moment alone anymore.

The phone vibrated on, undaunted by her lack of interest. Catherine almost shrugged. It couldn't be helped. Catherine thought about the freedom of not being able to do what was expected.

In an imperfect world, letting yourself be impolite was a rare and lovely pleasure.

It was probably only for ten minutes, but Catherine fell asleep twice, only to wake up each time in the panic that comes from being half naked with a back full of needles. Eventually, Harmison returned, took out the pins and reassessed.

'How's that feeling now?'

Catherine rotated her shoulder. 'Like nothing ever happened to it. That's amazing.'

'Well, that's great. The tenderness might return in the next few hours, but if you rest it I think you're good to go. Do let me know if you want a follow-up.'

'No that's great. Hey, if I do have any issues with energy, what would you recommend?'

'Probably with your make-up, a mix of ginseng, and ashwagandha.' He was writing out an invoice. 'If that doesn't work, I would look at aligning your energy through needling rather than herbs.'

Catherine thanked him and paid. Glad her shoulder no longer hurt, but pretty sure that was all she had gained out of this.

As she walked back through the gym, the same tiny man sporting a comb-over was pushing into a punching bag. The bag barely moved.

As she walked into the car park, she was surprised to pass another woman heading in. She was blonde and fit looking. She didn't look at Catherine at all. Which Catherine didn't mind, because the set of the blonde's jaw radiated anger. Someone, either the trainer, Harmison, or comb-over guy, was gonna get it.

Catherine rode home through misty rain that cut into her sense of being warm-blooded. Any feeling of peace that the needling had achieved was washed away in an Antarctic blast that was inside her jacket by the first set of lights. Ignoring the weather and the traffic, she thought about two things: what she would do next, and which country she could emigrate to as soon as she had cracked this mystery. The Pacific was lovely, but monotonous. Mexico could be interesting, but also could be very… *interesting.* Surely someone wanted hats in Vietnam. Surely.

As to what to do next, some research on herbs, background on the others in the troupe and a follow-up with Neal on the phone. The place starting with G, from that cryptic phone message, that was “all you'll ever need”. The thought brought a smile despite the rain.

She walked into the flat, mind buzzing, even if her nose was almost gone to frostbite. Boris counted the days of winter every year. Catherine looked at the date. July 5th. Not even half way, and already it had gone on forever. This is why she found day-counting daft. Not only do you completely miss the point of the beautiful moments, but you come up short every bloody time.

In minutes, the kettle was on. Catherine scratched Minty's leg as she dozed happily on the couch. Her shoulder did actually feel better, and it was still early, so she could get some work done, either on the mystery or on her day job.

She deliberated on muscle research or herb research. The latter reminded her of last summer. More herbs there, too. Was there a connection between Eastern medicine and murder? Or had it become so mainstream that more people had it in common now. Catherine reflected on all her cases, all the people, and wondered if any of them had never taken, say, Panadol, or a bath. Some things were so banal that they were simply assumed parts of being human in the 21st century on an island called Australia.

She had also been considering coffee, but since she was already getting a little tangential, she flicked open her cupboard of herbal teas. She poured out some jasmine balls, which a friend had brought her from Hong Kong, and wondered if they would be considered evidence if she were murdered.

Thunder rolled outside and she wondered if Boris was working the early shift. Ridiculous.

The phone rang. She jumped. Ridiculous.

'This is Catherine.'

The voice was deep and assuming. Like she should have heard of him. 'Catherine. I'm Anthony Barwick.'

'Hello, Anthony.'

He paused. He'd expected something different. 'You haven't heard my voicemail?'

'No. Sorry, busy day. Are you interested in a hat?' There was a sharp exhalation at the other end of the phone. Catherine knew she had misstepped, but had no idea why. She decided to coddle his silence.

'Catherine. My daughter died three days ago. Her name was Mia. You know her as Silver.'

'Ah.' Catherine changed gears. 'I'm sorry, Mr Barwick. Virginia did mention you would call.'

'Can you help me?' He sounded momentarily strangled.

'Mr Barwick.' Catherine kept her voice calm.

'Anthony. Why did I become "Mr Barwick"?'

'Because I first thought you were a hipster wanting a cool hat. Now you are the father of someone I saw die. I thought the honorific was warranted.'

Another long breath. 'You were there?'

'I was.'

'I didn't know that.'

Catherine sat on the couch. Minty rolled slightly in her sleep. 'Anthony. I'm already looking into this for Virginia.'

'I can pay.'

'There's also the police.'

'Yeah.' He grunted. 'That's why I want to pay. They won't talk to me.'

'What makes you think there's anything to talk about aside from an awful accident?'

'I have a feeling.'

Catherine looked out the window. She knew where this could go. 'Why do you think I would talk more than the police? Plus, I don't have their power, or their resources.'

'You're a free citizen. You can say things that won't mess up a court case. You don't have as many rules, and you're smart. That's what I've been told.'

'That doesn't mean I'll always tell you everything.'

Steel entered his voice. 'And you're a pain. I heard that too.'

Catherine shook her head. Who did these people talk to? 'Where are you based?'

'I live in Lakes Entrance, but I'm in town. I'm staying at the Rydges in Swanston Street. Will you come and see me?'

She rolled her eyes, but her voice remained professional. 'No. I have work to do. But you can come see me. 51a Albion Street, Brunswick. We can talk in my studio.'

'Where you make hats.'

'I'll put down the block and ribbons when you arrive. Come whenever before 4pm.'

'Thanks. I'll be there soon.'

'Is it just you?'

'What?'

'I know you're married. Is your wife with you?'

A pause. 'Jenny. No. She's back home. She can't be here right now. It's too hard.'

'Okay. I'm just working out who I'm talking to.'

He arrived just after 2pm. Catherine was momentarily surprised. She'd been focused on some crimson beadwork and had forgotten all other reality, which was why she liked making hats. Any job that can make winter, murder and time disappear is a worthy profession.

7

They have all the money in the world, all the food money can buy, and what do they do? Try and make more money. The tail's wagging the dog.
~Boris Shakhovskoy

Anthony Barwick was a big man. About fifty-five, with a shock of brown hair and a goatee beard flecked with greys. His body was broad in a way that indicated he liked the gym and his food in about the same proportion. His brown eyes were sharp, looking out over deep bags that indicated the sleepless nights that accompanied the violent death of a loved one.

Catherine opened the door and he nodded to her, entering without introduction before looking around the room. His eyes fixed on the poster of Audrey Hepburn, which was looking a little dog-eared. He looked at the hats in the window for ten seconds, with a silence that should have been awkward, but wasn't, at least to Catherine.

'Some beautiful work here.' He looked at her with a smile that seemed to come from much farther away.

'Are you a fan of fashion?'

'No. I started a business making and selling rigging twenty years ago. I don't have an eye for art. By the time I could afford this stuff, it was too late.'

He sounded like thousands of men who thought their ignorance of fashion was a virtue, but without the usual judgement. He seemed genuinely interested.

'You don't have to know about it to like it.'

'Then I like that one.' He pointed at a hard beret in silver. 'Mia would have loved it.'

'Have a seat. Tea?'

He smiled, which looked more like a wince. 'Anything stronger?'

She poured him a double scotch over ice, guessing correctly. Herself a gin. Sure it was ten past two, but grief doesn't care for norms, so neither did she.

He took a grateful sip, squared his shoulders, and started talking. Then stopped at the first word. Took a long breath, and another small sip.

'Mia. Mia was a lovely girl.' He paused. 'Always bright and happy. Swimming, netball, surfing. Just a great kid. Did well at school, never any trouble. She was the centre of a big family, the one we all loved.'

He was looking directly at her, rather than staring at a fixed point, which people often did when opening up to strangers.

'She started circus when she was twelve. Liked it more than gymnastics because it wasn't a competition. We encouraged it, of course. I was working sixty hours a week and didn't really know how to parent. It's amazing how the clichés come true: the father, so busy providing he misses being a father.

'When she was sixteen she came out to us. I was okay with it, even though I knew it would hurt my parents. I just wanted her to be happy. It took Jenny, my wife, a few weeks, but she was all right after that. Then Mia started drifting. Whether it was those weeks Jenny adjusted, or that I didn't mention it, or the influence of her first girlfriend – Kate was her name – I don't know.'

He drank another sip, bigger than Boris would take. 'She was the youngest of four. I knew what teenagers did. But it wasn't just a few drinks. She would come home without sleeping, or be so black midweek I knew she must have hit it hard. I tried to talk to her. She shut me out. Was okay with Jenny, but shut me out.'

'The day she turned twenty-one, she had access to an inheritance from her grandfather. A million bucks.' He sipped. 'She left that night for New York and didn't come back. I didn't even know she was in Melbourne until a few months ago, when a family friend saw her in town. She'd been here a year. No contact with her brothers, her Mum. I hadn't known if she was even alive.'

He looked at his feet. 'That's why I want to pay you. Because I need to know more than "we're following every possibility, Mr Barwick". I want to know. I want someone to pick up the phone when I call. I don't care if you've found nothing, I don't care if you've taken the day off. Just be honest with me and tell me what you're looking at. Can you do that?' He looked at her intently, but his words were soft. He wasn't begging.

Catherine sipped her gin. 'I'll be honest with you before you've paid me. Some things you should know. I sometimes find nothing. I won't look any harder than I already was for Virginia and you could probably find better use for your money elsewhere.'

'I know I sound like someone who just wants to buy his daughter back. And I know I can't. But I didn't have any information for three years, then I lost her for good. I just–' his voice suddenly caught. 'If you don't do it, I'll try. I'll try to find out and we both know I'll fail, Catherine. I've failed enough for a lifetime.'

'What do you mean by that, exactly?'

'I mean I lost Mia. I lost my only daughter. I want your help to know what happened to her. That's all.'

Catherine considered this. 'Then write a cheque, but take a hat too.'

He finished his scotch.

'Did any of your family possibly have contact with Silver in the past three years?'

'No.' He said it slowly. With a weight to it.

'Is it possible they might have, without you knowing?'

He stared hard at the floor. 'My family is happy, Catherine. The only thing that's been hard has been Mia not wanting to be a part of it.'

Catherine's heard a mantra in that. She imagined he said this every holiday, and more loudly after Silver left.

'Who was the family friend who saw Silver?'

'Mia.'

'Sorry, Mia. Who was the family friend?'

He stared, making a decision. 'A cousin of mine. Rob Barwick.'

'Does he live here?'

'No. He's from Metung. East Gippsland. He was down on business.'

'Where did he see her? Did they speak?'

He was standing now, and speaking more quickly. 'He saw her

outside Flagstaff Station. She was on her way to work in a cafe, he was going to court. Legal business stuff, nothing illegal.' He sniffed. 'If she was actually in court, I don't know what she was in for, and I haven't been able to find out. Rob says they spoke for about seven minutes. She told him she was working for the Ring Tail Circus and that she was living in Flemington. She had been back a year. Didn't get enough work in New York to live, so had to return.'

'That's a lot of detail.'

'I asked him about it several times. I needed to know everything.'

'Were you ever a cop?'

'No. Just a Dad who cared.' His face was almost completely still. Whatever he was feeling, he had worn it for a long time.

Stevie's wine glass was almost upright, not so much a toast as a talking stick. 'So I told her there was no way I would ever submit to a backwater Canberran and I dropped the file on the floor as I walked out.'

Catherine shook her head, leaning on the bar. 'Is that the third job you've rage-quit this year?'

'Only the second. You're thinking of that probation I didn't pass.'

Catherine was talking with Stevie at the bar while Boris rode the Friday night wave. People were three-deep at the bar and he maintained a continuous lumbering motion, making drinks and wiping spills while knowing instinctively who was next and who was being served by a colleague. Even without Stevie's hilarious tales of corporate self-sabotage, Catherine would have been entertained tonight. It was like watching an open fire, or a fine dancer, one that brought you a fresh drink every twenty minutes.

Stevie simpered, 'Any more sightings of that she-devil that was threatening Boris the other night?'

'Not by me. Though I haven't spoken to Boris all day. For all I know, they've been playing cat and mouse all afternoon.'

'What were you working on, Miss?'

Catherine sat straighter on her stool. 'Crimson hats and happy families.'

'Your own happy one?'

'No, no. You'll notice, Stevie, that I'm not drinking doubles, which is when you know Mother dearest has been involved. This was another happy family. They lost a daughter this week.'

'The circus kid?'

'Mmm.'

'Twenty three. That's a fucking shame.' They were silent a few moments. Stevie realised his Riesling had evaporated just as Boris passed him another and took his card from the bar.'

'That man really is a genius, isn't he?' Stevie rolled a cigarette and moved towards the back beer garden.

Twenty minutes later, the tide had subsided. Boris went to Catherine's corner.

'How was the day?'

'I think we need to learn more about Chinese herbs again.'

He grimaced. 'Oh dear. I remember not being great about that last time.'

'Oh well, just keep being good at being you. Stevie asked if Harley has stalked you further.'

'Not yet. Though the hairs haven't quite touched the back of my neck again. It's only been a night.'

Boris leaned against the coffee machine. For a man who could run like the wind and fight like a lion when required, he was remarkably puffed by a busy service.

Catherine said, 'So I'm getting well paid suddenly.'

'Sell a few hats?' Boris continued to scan for more customers.

'No, the Silver issue. Her Dad came to see me.'

'Oh yeah, Virginia said that would happen.'

'He's all about money.'

Boris rolled his eyes. It wasn't that he judged people for being all about money. It just wasn't an option to him, or it would all be about not very much. 'And giving it to us?'

'Yeah, but he'll want a pound of flesh. Wants all the information, all the time.'

'So he's bought us?'

'No, he's bought the right to have his calls answered, at a premium too.'

'Did you explain you were already working on it, and that it could just be an accident?'

'Yes, he's across all that. And while I'm not sure about murder, that little scene at Silver's flat tells me there's something going on. As for Barwick, I think he just wants to feel like he's doing something.'

'It amazes me that some men feel like "doing something" is paying someone else to do something.'

Boris lumbered off to serve a pint. Catherine weighed up the potential of another gin before home. After twenty eight seconds of deliberation, she decided it was in the best interests of the planet to have another under her belt before she went out in the cold. It was one of the dead nights of winter where the absence of any warmth started to soak into your bones. About this time every year, a good many of Melbourne's five million strong citizenship asked why the hell they had chosen to live there, even if the footy was interesting. She waved at Boris, who nodded.

She flicked through her phone and stopped at an article about Silver's death. While not mentioning her name, the circus accident had caused a media stir. There was a quote from Virginia and it mentioned that a report would be made for the coroner.

For a moment Catherine wondered if it would have been worth staying in the force all those years ago, so she could have had access to the toxicology report. Then Boris put her drink down in front of her and she realised that if she had to front up to work at a police station tomorrow, she would worry about staying out too late.

Millinery, on the other hand, she could do no matter how little she'd slept. Plus, it was fun, hardly anyone shot at you, and late nights were actively encouraged.

She toasted her own good health. Some decisions get even better as the years go on.

Boris had walked a hundred metres towards home before he realised he hadn't been watching his back. He immediately spun around, but saw nothing. No one dived behind a lamp post or huddled against a wall. He saw only the muted lights of midnight in Brunswick. As he walked on, he came to the path that ran parallel to the train line. His hands became fists within his coat pockets. He slowed and looked both ways. The path was well lit towards the city, with Anstey Station pouring yellow light across the path. Even at this hour. The path north – his way home – was almost pitch dark for the next 100 metres before the lonely lamp posts started again. Maybe this was why the council rates went up as you got closer to the city.

He walked, eyes darting, treading softly so he could hear any footsteps. He heard them, and leaned back against the wall, pretending to check his phone. A big man passed him without a look. Boris waited a full minute until the figure turned off into Tinning Street, and wondered if he ever wouldn't feel this dread nibbling at him.

He moved on slowly, keeping himself as even as he could. He knew that if he gave in and ran he would be puffed quickly and likely unable to shake the terror that he could feel on the edge of his skin, just trying to prick its way in. He hugged the railway side of the path as he came to Peveril Street. The wheat silo blocked any light from the block beyond.

Boris saw a figure, the same man, walking back to the rail path. Boris walked on in a steady pace. He was hardly breathing. He scoured the area for a second attacker. Sweat cooled on the back of his neck, even in the damp cold. He looked back once: the man was five metres behind. Cozens Street was fifty metres ahead. He could head up it. He moved faster. Then the sound came, and the dread bit hard.

The footsteps behind him quickened. Footfalls turned into the thump of a run up. Boris spun and took the knee. The man was on top of him, eyes wide on a moustachioed face, fist raised. Boris sprang upward and forward, his shoulder slamming into the man's chest like a hammer. The man made a strangled howl as he fell against the opposite brick wall and slid down. Boris stood back, fists up, checking for the next assailant. When they failed to appear he pressed his advantage, moving towards the gasping man.

The man waved a business card as if it was a white flag.

Boris snatched it up, his action hard and swift, reading it as he caught his breath.

'Anthony Barwick. You're Silver's dad?'

The man nodded. Clutching his chest.

'What the hell are you playing at?'

Barwick could only wheeze. Boris looked both ways along the path. No one was around, though he could hear the last train from town approaching.

Barwick clutched his chest. Sweat was visible on his head. Boris checked the path again. Both ways. Nothing coming.

'Jesus.' He held out a hand.

The panting man came up, grasping Boris's shoulder, before leaning against the wooden fence between the path and the railway.

The train came closer. The white lights pierced the gloom followed by the yellow of the windows. Boris counted the faces in the windows as the train slowed into the station. Thirteen. Eight women, five men.

Barwick collected his breath. Boris rotated his shoulder.

'I'm sorry. That was stupid.'

Boris could smell bourbon in the air. 'What were you trying to do? Scare me?'

'I hear you can handle yourself. I was just going to follow you and see if you noticed. But then I, I.'

'What?'

Boris realised the man was crying. Violence then tears. Exasperated, Boris turned his face up towards indifferent clouds.

After checking again for Harley or her goons, Boris awkwardly approached the sobbing Barwick. Barwick's tears gleamed on his cheeks in the pale light of the nearby lamppost. For a second Boris worried he'd hurt him badly. Waiting on an ambulance would be a perfect way to spend his night. Then Barwick shuddered twice and whispered, 'Mia.'

'Easy mate.'

Barwick, his open face lined, his voice hoarse, said, 'I've been waiting three years for her to just knock on the door one day.'

Boris stood close, still aware of any movements around them. He thought he saw something on the other side of the tracks; stared hard for a few seconds. Nothing. He wasn't entirely sure it wasn't a ruse. He could smell a powerful amount of liquor on Barwick's breath.

'I always imagined,' Barwick continued, 'she'd come in and hold her mother. Then she'd find me and I could tell her it was okay, that we were her parents. That she was safe.'

This sent him off into further sobs. It was a short squall, and a few minutes later he was breathing deeply. Composing himself as Boris kept vigilant.

In the time-honoured tradition of Aussie blokes everywhere, Barwick shook off the emotion and straightened his back. Moving on to business.

'I understand you're the muscle?'

'Well, more a friend. But yeah. Why try and hit me?'

'Stupid idea. Just wanted to see how good you were. I like to know where I'm spending my money.' He took a few more deep breaths. 'And maybe I've just wanted to hit someone for days and, I thought… I don't know. I'm sorry.'

Boris regarded him for a long time. He remembered his father telling him not to assume someone was clever just because they were rich. It seemed apt at the moment.

'You could have just spoken to me.'

'Well.' Barwick smiled wanly. 'I am.'

'Is anyone watching this?'

Barwick shook his head, but checked the opposite side of the tracks. 'No. Just me being stupid.'

'Anything else you need to know? I'm keen to not be outside.' Boris checked around again. No one about, but he was aware that talking to Barwick was distracting him,

'Is she trustworthy?'

'Who?'

'Kint.'

Boris blinked in the cold. 'You sneak up on me, try to hit me, now you're asking for dirt on my best friend?'

'It's been a big day.'

'Get some rest.'

Boris walked into the night, even after he heard a sob. He didn't look back, but he wanted to solve the crime, because Mia was a person and people loved her. Catherine would do this, he knew, and suddenly the fear of a few minutes ago was worth feeling. His blood was up. There was no more fear. Now he was just waiting for the bitter taste of adrenaline to leave his mouth and almost hoping for Harley to come out of a shadow.

He also knew this feeling would be fleeting, so he kept moving.

The night was eerily still, with only the faintest of hums from Sydney Road, four hundred metres east. Boris took a last look around before he entered his street through an alleyway. He hadn't planned to use the alley, but there was something so stupid about doing it he figured his potential captors would have jettisoned any ideas about cornering him there. This paranoia was exhausting. He had to think twelve times more than usual.

The lock of the door behind him gave him less solace than he had hoped. He even felt strange in the house. He could hear his housemate's television in their room, and knew from the sound which episode of Star Trek they were up to. The kitchen seemed empty, and was. Boris opened the fridge and took out a beer.

He didn't open it until he had checked every room of the house.

He flopped on the couch and opened the can. He was still shaking his head at Barwick. He took out his phone and texted Catherine.

'Barwick attacked me on the way home. Said he was testing me.'

His phone chirped seconds later. 'What? That's crazy. I didn't even mention you. I guess Virginia must have described us as a package deal.'

'Well he knew me. I'm fine, btw.'

Catherine's text came back with a rolled eyes emoji. 'I assumed as much. But if you want me to fawn over you and check your temperature, pop round.'

He humphed a small laugh. 'No. I'm buggered and have been looking over my shoulder all day. Harley's goons are probably better fighters than Barwick.'

'What a strange man. His money landed, I'll send your share through, you've earned it more than me today.'

'Thanks. Any new leads? I want to solve this quickly.'

'Nothing since an hour ago, though I've just been lying on the couch listening to jazz and trying to remember that spring will come one day.'

'Just count the days.'

'It's July dear. That's like waiting for Christmas in February. Didn't you listen to anything Yoda said about living in the moment?'

'I don't think he ever said anything about that. Do you mean "do or do not, there is no try"?'

'Similar sentiment dear. Just live in the now.'

Boris stretched and tried to make his back crack. It didn't work. 'Okay, you be in the moment with Hancock. I'm gonna get to bed. Talk tomorrow.'

'Sweet dreams, my prince x.'

8

There are many ways to tell a story; mine is the other way.
~Ciara Beretta

The whine of the engine hurt Boris' head. He winced in the pale morning light. His whole body felt unclean, despite the shower he'd stepped out of moments ago. Stress, that was the thing. When you spent your whole day looking over your shoulder, you looked forward to being in your own house, with the lights off and the door double locked. It made you want to elongate that moment, so you didn't go to bed. You enjoyed feeling safe, and before you knew it you'd had half a bottle of scotch and fallen asleep on the couch with a comic on your chest, again.

His reflection in the rear view mirror was tired and looked both regretful and regrettable. Whatever his best self was, this wasn't it.

He would do some meditation after he dropped off the car, that was his promise. If he could get even halfway to the void through this foggy, aching head, that would be a morning well spent. Or, alternatively, there was the prospect of a massive fry-up. He would certainly need more coffee. He took the Melville Road way to the mechanic. On one side of the street were parks and the odd oval studded with the brave outlines of junior footy players lining up for warm-ups before their match. On the other was a variation on the theme of the West Brunswick family home: white fence, brown fence, weatherboard, brick. So many houses, so many stories.

Why had he felt the need to read Batman comics at 3am?

Feeling his failure at life deep in his skin, he turned into Dawson Street and started looking for the mechanic. Squinting as the sun momentarily broke through the black clouds. 'A normal person would have put the phone on to navigate.'

The garage was open for business, according to both the open garage doors and the flashing colourful sign that had cheered exactly no one up in its entire existence. Boris pulled in and got out of the car. A middle aged man with a hundred-year-old face walked up to him. 'Yis?' he asked in a Mediterranean accent that Boris equated with Brunswick's fast-receding working class history.

'I'm Boris, I've brought my car in for a service.'

'Why today?' the man was grinning in a way that made Boris' skin feel even worse.

'Someone told me the best mechanic you've got works Saturdays.'

The grin intensified. 'Oh, right. You him, uh.'

'Who?'

'You're Boris.' The voice came from behind him, as someone walked out of the garage. 'The man who picks people up in the rain, even if they might be a psycho. I told my Uncle Albert all about you.'

Boris eyed Jolene, aghast. No one had ever looked so beautiful in coveralls. Ever.

He smiled as it started raining.

Catherine was barely on her second cup of coffee when her phone rang. Virginia.

Catherine didn't so much roll her eyes as check to see her halo was intact as she answered sweetly. 'Happy Saturday to you dear Gin.'

'Darling, I'm sorry. I've been with the police again.'

Catherine kept her tone light as she braced herself for the psychic onslaught. 'Oh really? I wonder sometimes. The same ones?

'No, plainclothes this time.'

'Oh, I see. They're officially investigating her death, then?'

'Yes, and so I told them. I told them everything, about the bitchiness, the rivalries, Harley, the lot. I can't protect them anymore, fuck them all.' She sounded low and her words were taut.

Catherine's neck prickled. 'That's an about-turn in a few days. Aside from the politics, how would we know that there was any foul play?'

'What do you think?'

Catherine knew well what she thought, but that didn't interest her at that moment. 'I think I'm not sure. But *you* sound sure.'

'I think they know there were things going wrong, and maybe Silver's death was a result of that. I fear they may blame me, for negligence, or something. They talked about a toxicity report.'

'Toxicology?'

'That too.'

Catherine did roll her eyes at that one.

'And?'

'They asked about Silver's herbs.'

Catherine was on her feet now, moving to the window. 'Poison?'

'They think it might have been. There were downers in her system, maybe sleeping tablets. They weren't entirely sure, because it was all mixed up with the underlying stuff. Silver was using coke and speed and another thing I've never heard of.'

'Why are you telling me this?'

'Because your brief has changed. It's no longer to find out what happened; it's to keep me safe.'

Blood drained from Catherine's face. 'Safe, from poisoning?'

'No dear. Safe from the police. They're circling.'

Suddenly Catherine needed air. She found her slippers and went to the balcony. 'But you've done nothing wrong.'

'Of course not,' she replied. Too quickly. 'Nothing at all. But I'm a woman in the arts dear, and you know what that means. The police will always hate me.'

Cars were moving slowly up Albion Street. Catherine wanted to be in one. 'That's not enough to defame you or anything else you may be worried about.'

'Maybe they'll find something else then.'

'Virginia, if you know something and need to tell me, come over and we will talk right now. Because if you have done something wrong, I will find out. So will the police if they're now investigating'

'No,' the answer came too quickly again. 'I'm busy. I have to work things out here. The classes start again on Monday. I have to sort out the training roster.'

'You know where I am.'

'I know, and I appreciate it.'

Catherine paused. 'Oh, one more thing Virginia, was the plainclothes officer a somewhat haughty blonde woman?'

'No, a short man, with a ridiculous moustache.'

'Right, okay, good to know.'

The call finished and Catherine had the distinct feeling she was being paid by two people who wanted to know what happened to Silver, or Mia, for all the wrong reasons. This was where the job became like everyone else's – a series of lines you wouldn't cross, all laid out for you.

Catherine went back inside and closed the door, a little too hard.

The knock on the door was tentative and Catherine wondered: client? Barwick? Virginia? Which of these wanted to see her, but not enthusiastically enough to knock with conviction.

'Boris. That's a very unmanly knock from you.'

'I thought you might be sleeping. I was hedging my bets.'

Catherine toasted him with the large mug she was holding as if it were evidence of her early rising nature. 'It's 10.15 my darling. Even I have some standards some days. '

'You weren't happy with me last week.'

'Ah, but you weren't to know that last week the world decided that Thursday night was so full of promise that I had to stay out in the magical mist. Whereas last night, although called Friday, was really just Tuesday morning in a funny hat.'

Boris smiled, looking at his shoes. 'Well, you'd know.'

She made room for him to enter. 'I don't make funny hats, I make fabulous hats.'

'Indubitably.'

'So what brings you here and why are you in such a good mood? For a man attacked last night you're practically glowing.'

'Well, sir stayed up too late drinking scotch and we seem to be getting paid by everyone, so I thought we could spend some dosh on a fry-up.'

'That is a good plan, especially if it involves mushrooms. But that's not enough. You've got your Shakhovskoy Goes Forth aura on. Did Ciara confess her undying love to you?'

Boris's face heated. 'No. Just someone I gave a lift to the other day surprised me.'

Catherine flicked an eyebrow and drained her coffee. 'Tell your story walking, pal. I'm hungry.'

Forty five minutes later, Boris was briefed on the arrival of plainclothes police on the issue, and Catherine was feeling full to bursting while Boris finished off the last of his big breakfast. The café was warm, until someone walked in or out, which was only one minute in every three. Catherine decided to take that as a win. Besides, the music in the café was one of her favourite jazz albums – a welcome break from those two awful words "ambient beats" – and she found herself bopping the tines of her fork against her little finger. She was tossing up whether to order another coffee or a bottle of champagne, for in such a dreary week, someone flirting with Boris was worthy of revels that would wake the gods.

'"How do you know I'm not a psycho?" That's almost peak Boris, that one.'

Boris's eyes flashed happy. 'We shouldn't make a big deal out of it. The car will probably cost zillions.'

'Such worries are not for us this week. Usually, I know you worry about bills but this week you're rich.'

'I just have to worry about Harley and her goons, or Barwick.'

Catherine pointed her fork. 'Yes well. Your bravery and bulk earned you that there hash brown so don't get too morbid. Now Boris, are you working tonight?'

'Not till 4. Wanna go to the zoo?'

'No.' She gave him a hard look, which he ignored. 'I think we should day drink. It's not raining, I want to think about the case, but not sober, the police can do that, and you've been smiled at by a pretty girl.'

'What about picking up my car?'

'You can do that Monday, surely?

His flickering smile was the one that came at the start of his romantic cycle. 'Ah, I think I might wanna go pick it up today.'

'Ah yes, of course. I was thinking of my needs, not your own. Yes, you should go and swoon at the young lady. Then come to mine for some champers. I just feel like it's a day to waste in the most beautiful way possible.'

Boris had to admit it was tempting. He could sleep for an hour and get through a shift easily enough. Though the idea of ducking a punch while tipsy didn't appeal. He chased a mushroom around the plate as he weighed his options. Then the phone rang.

'Hello.'

'Boris, it's your favourite mechanic.'

'Hello Jolene.'

Catherine made vomiting sounds on the other side of the table.

'What is that?' asked Jolene.

Boris stood quickly. 'Sorry Jolene, I'm just visiting a leper colony and need to get outside.'

Catherine started sighing loudly. 'Check my oil Boris, oh, work the shaft.' Boris gave her the finger as the café door creaked shut behind him. Catherine flashed him a smile and stole his last hash brown.

'Sorry, with you now. How's the car?'

'New fan belt, new brakes, good as new. Really needs a clean.'

'Ah, yeah, sorry I would have if I–' Boris let the line die the painful death it deserved.

'You can come pick it up any time before 12.30.'

Boris grinned, doing up his jacket with his free hand. 'Ripper. I'll come now.'

Boris waved at Catherine, who looked pained and made a money sign with her finger and thumb. Boris answered with a single finger as Jolene replied, 'The lepers will be ok?'

'Entropy, you know? Things fall apart, but this one keeps coming back together.'

For the second time in two days, Boris realised he wasn't checking his surroundings. He'd been wandering down Victoria Street thinking about Jolene and had forgotten for a second that he was at any stage about to run into a very angry Harley, a very burly henchman or both. He scanned the area. Kids playing soccer, people walking dogs, everyone enjoying the fact that it wasn't raining. No one too tough looking anywhere. Maybe she wasn't interested any more. Maybe Dodgy Kevin had done the trick.

His grin died as he heard the roar of a motorcycle scream past. Boris didn't quite jump, but he was far from disinterested. There was no way they would disappear for long. Everything he knew about Harley said that she wasn't the quitting type. They could come at any time. He flexed his shoulder, a little stiff after his altercation with Barwick. He walked across the wide and visible expanse of Clifton Park and into the wooded grove of Gilpin Reserve beyond it.

It was one of the stranger parks in Brunswick, pertaining to a different time, when thick trees and less play equipment were *de jour*. Not much was happening today aside from a hipster band making a cheap film clip. Boris was amused, but certainly not intimidated by them. It was a rule he had noticed: people who can't dance are usually useless fighters. He breathed out and noticed that he couldn't see his own breath. Things were definitely looking up.

Turning into Dawson Street, he could see his Ford on the street near the garage. A quick look inside confirmed that no effort had been made on Jolene's part to tidy it at all – this was good news. She was either not trying to save him or change him, or she was just pragmatic and didn't want to stick her hand into whatever was in the pile of crap.

As he approached the garage he ran a hand through his hair, then caught sight of his reflection in the window and gave up. The double garage doors were up now, but the colourful light still screamed "open".

Jolene was seated behind a desk when he walked in. She smiled and Boris realised this was a huge day of firsts for his interactions with a mechanic.

He gestured to the car outside. 'How'd did it go?'

'It's running and you won't have to worry about that banshee wail anymore.'

'It, ah.' Boris rubbed his chin. 'It actually wasn't worrying me too much.'

'Hmm.'

'Should it?'

'Well,' she leaned back. 'You should always worry about new noises on a machine that could crash, so you saying it didn't worry you means you either have other things to worry about–'

'Or?' he prompted.

'You are very stupid.'

Boris grinned. 'Well, that's not really a binary option.'

She started writing out the invoice. 'So you plead both?'

'Yes, your honour. Now treat me as you would a very dumb friend and take all my money.'

Her hand slowed. 'Ah yes. Do me a favour and make sure that door's closed.'

Boris hadn't even seen the door behind him, presumably leading to the garage itself. A mechanical bang presented as audio evidence a second later, to confirm his suspicion.

'So it's $200 for the fan belt. $150 for the brakes and $135 for labour.'

'Right.' Boris swallowed a sigh and got out his wallet.

'Or $100 bucks and you take me to dinner next week.'

'What?'

Her voice grew breathy and businesslike, as if she were suppressing a yawn. 'Dinner. It's the third meal of the day for most of us, taken in the evening. I like mine to involve a starch or pasta of some kind.' She cleared her throat. 'And please say something because I'm kinda out on a limb here. If I've misread you and you're married you can pay the $485 and I'll apologise.'

Her face was now almost completely pink. Boris closed his mouth, which was hanging slightly open. 'Yes, of course. Dinner. I know the concept and like it and, like–' he waved like a very tired queen, '– you.'

She exhaled audibly. 'Oh good. I thought you were about to tell me about your wife.'

'Oh, can't she come?'

'Boris!'

He grinned. 'No wife, no girlfriend, no dog. Just me.'

There was a silence between them as they gathered their thoughts. Boris was desperate to say something, but the only line he could think of was "we seem to have covered a lot of ground" and even he knew not to say that. As if sensing the moment, the lights briefly dimmed.

'So, $100?' Jolene found her tongue first.

Boris jolted to action. 'Oh yes, right. I, um.' He took out his wallet and scratched for his credit card. 'I work nights. Um, I'm free on Tuesday?'

She winced. 'Can't do Tuesday. Karate.'

Boris nodded. 'Cool, useful hobby. Ahh, what about a late supper? I finish at 11?'

'I'm a morning person.'

He nodded. 'Okay, let me try and sort something out. How's tomorrow?'

'Done.'

'Great. I'll swap some shifts around.'

She grinned. 'Glasgow Palace, right?'

'Yep. For my sins.'

'Good parma. But let's not go there.'

'No, let's decidedly not.'

She took out her phone. 'What's your number?'

He gave it and she rang him.

'Got it, so tomorrow, provided I can get off the shift, I'll call you with a plan before 4?'

She sat back in her chair. 'Sounds good. I can see you make good plans.'

'Well. That's debatable, but more on that tomorrow.'

'See ya, Boris.'

As he left, he checked the walls but saw nothing out of the ordinary: calendars with cars on them and a coke machine in the corner. It was definitely a mechanic's garage. He wasn't being pranked and it wasn't another dimension. He walked out into the street and felt full and satisfied and excited and almost safe.

Behind him, Jolene changed the radio station to suit herself, to catch the PBS jazz shows. He got in his car and then sang all the way to Sydney Road and would probably have made it singing all the way to Catherine's house had he not received the text message. Group text, to him and Catherine. From Neal.

'I've got the phone going, only partially, but I think you'll agree it's worth a look.'

Boris leaned back in the seat and cracked his neck. 'One, two, three, f–' His phone started ringing. He answered it.

'Shall I pick you up, or will you meet me there?'

Forty minutes later, Boris, Catherine, and Neal were hunched over the grey android phone that once belonged to Silver. Over the previous twenty minutes, Catherine and Boris had watched Neal make a cup of tea, discussed trimesters with June, and made unsuccessful calls to Ciara, so they made the executive decision to crack on.

Neal slid his fingers to adjust the messages flashing on the screen. 'We can see the thirteen messages that Silver received on this phone.

We can't see what she wrote back, or any internet data. I'm sorry. I'm working on it. This looks like it would have been a burner to her. She didn't use it much. Plus, it's an old model.'

Boris frowned. 'Why does a single person need a burner? I thought that was just for affairs?'

Neal's eyes were warm and he sounded as amused as ever. 'That's your trusting nature again, Boris. Also, maybe someone was looking at her phone? It doesn't seem like trust was in abundance at the troupe.'

Even though the day was dark outside, Neal's office was well lit with a gentle yellow glow coming from his antique overhead lamp, augmented by the thin sunlight coming through the two windows. Neal handed an A4 printout to Boris and a printout plus the phone to Catherine, instinctively knowing that she would want the primary source, too. 'Here you are, these are the thirteen messages that I've been able to decipher. I don't have dates or times and I can't at all access the phone's sent items that would fill in a lot of the gaps.'

Catherine looked down at her printout. Neal had double-spaced the messages for ease of reading.

> How can you say that?
>
> Don't listen to the chatter, you know they talk because they're jealous
>
> Ok
>
> I just want to wrap you up and make you mine forever
>
> Where's the coffee?
>
> You should be careful on the second twist, after that it's easy, but you know what happens if you overthink it. J
>
> I don't care about that anymore.
>
> Don't call me loser, I had enough of that as a kid

It was all those times I used ladders from cellars

I can still smell you on myself. I'll never wash this off.

You've hurt me once too often.

I thought I could trust you.

Adios.

'Where's the *Everything you need, and ever could need, is in the ga–'* she asked Neal.

'As I said, there is data missing, and that message has disappeared too. I didn't want to put it on the same sheet, as now it appears to have gone. I was wondering if it was a bizarre screenshot or something.'

'That doesn't seem right, but I'll discount nothing at this stage. Boris, first thoughts?'

Boris read the messages; read them again.

'At this stage, nothing. Unless they really liked coffee and never found it, so walked out.'

Catherine's face was blank.

'I know, it sounded better in my head.'

He read it again. He couldn't see a thread. This didn't clear anything up for him. Both Neal and Catherine were still reading, so, Boris read them again, lest he look like he wasn't concentrating enough. Next time he looked up, Neal was staring out of the window at the gathering storm. He caught Boris's eye and smiled politely, which could have meant anything, because Neal's primary setting was polite. He joined Neal in looking at the clouds, a dark swirl of nimbostratus heavy with imminent rain.

Boris worked out how many more days of winter remained. It didn't improve his mood at all. Even in his heavy jacket (Neal hadn't offered to take it) he felt damp and cool, despite his quiet joy about Jolene and dinner.

Catherine was still scowling at the phone a few minutes later, one foot slightly in front of the other: the dancer's pose she sometimes fell into when she was thinking. She pointed. 'It's this one that leaps out to me: "You should be careful on the second twist, after that it's easy, but you know what happens if you overthink it". That tells me it's a circus connection'

Boris nodded. 'Or at the very least someone who spoke the lingo, or knew the world. Either another acrobat–'

'Or someone like Virginia who knows circus. Let's not jump to conclusions, though.'

There was a roll of thunder a long way off as winter agreed with her.

Boris asked his question. 'When *I* have more than one message on my screen I can only see the latest one. Why did we see the "Everything you need" one? Shouldn't we only have been able to see 'Adios'?'

Neal's chin rose a few degrees. 'Just in case there weren't enough variables, I'm not entirely sure the messages are even in order. This phone seems to have been scrambled. Either by accident or by design. The other possibility is that we can't see that initial message.'

'It reads like the messages have been sent from different people.' Boris pointed to his sheet. '"I just want to wrap you up" quickly turns into "Don't call me loser". That seems tempestuous.'

'No.' Catherine's eyes didn't leave the phone screen. 'It's one person, but it's a romantic or intense relationship. And there's not much emotional regulation.'

'So someone young?'

'Not necessarily. Plenty of fifty year olds who can't regulate going round,' she added dismissively.

'What do you think?'

Catherine looked at Boris. 'It tells me someone was close to Silver, someone loved and disliked her simultaneously and that someone was also into the herbs, or something like it, if the germs text rings true.'

'The germs text?' Neal asked.

Boris smiled a little awkwardly. 'I workshopped "All you need is in the germs" as a possibility. I know a lot of people talk about gut flora these days.

Neal sniffed. 'Not the stupidest thing I've heard.' His expression indicated it was close.

Boris cleared his throat and shuffled his feet. He noticed for the first time that Neal had a small heater behind him and moved closer to it.

Neal clicked his tongue. 'No names, no initials. No nicknames.'

'Yes.'

'That seems less than useful.'

Catherine flashed a momentary grin. 'Doesn't it? But maybe that tells us something too.'

'Like what?'

'Well, read, if you please, your last four texts to June.'

Neal blinked at the unusual request. He took out his phone.

'"I'll come to bed soon. Two overs until tea" is the first. "I'm so looking forward to meeting our mutual friend: is the next. "Rice, cornflakes, tea and raspberry yoghurt" the third, and the fourth I'm vetoing.'

Catherine grinned. 'Did you address her, if I may, in that last one as "June" or any other identifiable name?'

'I did not.'

'Why not?'

'Because I am her husband and she knows who I am. It's also implied, heavily, in our marital contract that I know who she is. Hence I don't text her saying "Hello June, it's Nealamber, please buy some raspberry yoghurt".'

Catherine winked at Boris. 'See, so it implies only intimacy. Quite like the capricious nature of the messages.'

Boris nodded. 'Right. I couldn't see it, but now I do.'

'You're single, it would seem odd.'

'Last I checked, you're single too.'

'Yes but I've learned to live in other people's heads at the same time I inhabit my own.'

'Sounds exhausting.'

'Hence my love of gin, dear.' She handed the phone back to Neal. 'Great. Will you keep bashing away at the other side of the conversation?'

'I will.'

'What about other data? Internet usage? Social media? Bluetooth?'

'Bluetooth is on, but no devices listed. I haven't been able to find any internet or socials or even email. It's like this phone was being used for a single purpose.'

'Right, so it's just a burner, possibly to communicate with someone she couldn't talk to on her other phone,' suggested Catherine

Neal rubbed his chin. 'So, something clandestine from her usual life.'

'I've been told Silver was using drugs. Maybe there's a code here. Though I must say, it's elaborate.'

'Yep,' said Boris. 'I thought references to ladders and cellars was pretty clever.'

Neal stared at Boris. Boris elaborated. 'Ladders go up, like cocaine does, and cellars bring you down, like barbiturates.'

'I'll stick with raspberry yoghurt.'

Catherine interjected. 'I think you're both uncomplicated men and I'm glad to know you. Other people have things to hide.'

Boris smiled his thanks. 'Do you think people in the troupe would actually look at each other's phones? How?'

'I guess you don't take it up a tissu with you?'

'Still seems strange to me. Plus there's so much variance in the messages, it's a lot of work for a bag of coke.'

Neal rubbed a cheek. 'A clandestine lover then?'

'Or.' Catherine bit her lower lip. 'Knowing what I now know about Silver's family, I wonder if it's a sibling or someone she's estranged from.'

'"I want to wrap you up and make you mine"?'

'Does sound a bit creepy now you mention it.' She blinked. 'What about the fingerprints? Anything there?'

'Ah yes. I know two of them, they're on my file.'

Catherine and Boris made eye contact sheepishly.

'The other two aren't on anyone's. Certainly no ones I could hack. And I'm pretty good at that. These people have never had cause to be fingerprinted by Victoria's, or anywhere else's, finest.'

'Ugh. Okay. More questions than answers.'

'The title of your autobiography I am sure, dear Catherine.'

9

I don't worry about the next minute, I just know in this one I'm immortal.
~Harley

Boris couldn't hear the bar noise. He was immune to it. Alyce had taken his next day's shift and that meant this time tomorrow he would be looking at Jolene and she probably wouldn't be wearing overalls. If she was, he didn't think he'd mind. He pulled the tap and just for a moment all other thoughts left him. He was unaware of anyone called Silver, Ciara or even Catherine.

He didn't even know his own name, which was why the Four Pines XPA pint had the perfect amount of foam. Not that the hipster buying it had any appreciation. Boris did though, and as he worked the till, he was complete.

Until Catherine interrupted his thoughts. 'What would your phone say about you?'

'Probably what every girlfriend I've ever had would say: lose weight, be more interesting, spend less time with Catherine.'

'It amazes me that you assume your phone would side with those disappointing women.'

'Mum says the same thing. Though she also wants me to work in an office.'

'She wants grandchildren and knows that kids are expensive. It's an entirely different motivation. Also, she knows you're interesting.'

'She has to find me interesting, or it's no grandkids for her.'

'But your millions of texts, emails, what story would it tell?'

'I don't know. I use a lot of emoji's and spend too much time trying to find funny stuff online.'

'So what speech would it give at your sixtieth?'

He rolled his eyes, but considered it anyway. After a few seconds he spoke. 'He wanted to be amused. He had the keys to all knowledge but loved spaceships more than actual information.'

Catherine was impressed at the honesty. 'I could imagine much worse.'

'What would yours say?'

'She smiled when men texted back, she enjoyed life, but I could tell it was because she was trying to make a point.'

'Deep.'

'Reading dead people's text messages gets me there.'

'Hence the move away from gin?'

'Yes, it's red wine all the way tonight. Top me up, barkeep.'

Boris poured her a generous one and added it to her tab. 'What's your feeling?'

'There's not a lot to know, let alone to make a feeling, so I guess my feeling is stuck at curious. Bloody Barwick was a classic, though. I gave him the report and he went totally quiet, like it was a breakthrough.'

'You think it meant something to him?'

'I think he really likes feeling whatever power he has.'

Boris leaned back, a moment of sloth, that according to barkeep law would invite customers to come and take him away from his non-industry. 'All the messages seem pretty banal, aside from the twist one. I mean sure, "adios" at the end is menacing, but only because we know she died. If I texted you adios you'd think I was just saying seeya.'

'Most things are mundane until they aren't. Most murders aren't planned. It's a normal day and people are thinking about bringing the bins in, then someone, somehow, is dead.'

'Switch back to gin.'

Catherine popped a Cheezel. 'Don't feel bad, everyone pretends death isn't part of life until we're forced to face reality. That's why we've been so skittish since Tuesday.'

'I've been calm the past two days, and I've been attacked.'

'Well, there's exceptions and then there's rules right? Here she is.'

Ciara walked in, Boris smiled at her and then frowned as a group of football players walked in after her.

Ciara sat by Catherine. 'You unlocked the phone?'

'Yes, here's the list of texts.'

Ciara shook off her wet puffer jacket, hooked it on the hat stand and blew on her hands. She took the stool to Catherine's left.

Catherine passed the printout and watched Ciara perfunctorily stare at the page with almost no reaction. Which meant one of two things. 'Have you been sleeping?'

Ciara smiled wanly and shook her head. 'All I can hear is the silence from the others. I think they're talking about me.'

'Did Virginia say that the police were in touch with her again?'

Ciara looked at Catherine, her mouth tightening. 'No, she did not tell me anything.' She turned away.

Catherine felt a pang in her gut. Ciara was an outsider. Catherine knew that pain.

'You haven't heard from any of them?'

'Only a call from Jean. She's the most free of Harley. Not much from the others at all.'

'Boris.' Catherine called, thinking to get Ciara a bourbon, but he was only a quarter through the first round of the football team's order and didn't look like he was going to get any back-up from his colleagues. Catherine shrugged. Good things came to those who wait at the Palace.

Catherine touched the page with the messages. 'Before we talk more on this, I need to ask you a difficult question. Did you know Silver was using drugs?'

Ciara's eyes fell away. She nodded imperceptibly.

'Why didn't you tell me this earlier?'

Ciara's face creased. She went to speak, couldn't, tried again. 'I'm sorry. I should have. It's just.' There was a pause.

'When I'm spending my time working out how someone died, I shouldn't have to find out a bit of info like that from the cops. Not when you must have known.' Catherine's voice was even. Her eyes were fixed. Ciara was looking at her again.

'Ok. I'm sorry.' She pinched her nose. 'We all knew. She said she had stopped. I believed her.' She tapped the bar. "I wanted to believe, that's why I didn't say. It was my heart thinking, not my head.'

'You realise that it could look like she was high and that's what caused her death.'

'Yes.'

Catherine wondered if the woman had slept even half a night since Silver's death. 'Anything else I should know?'

'You know we were an item.'

'Yes.'

'Then no.' She held her hand out on the bar, Catherine took it. It was cool. 'Catherine, I'm sorry. I've told you everything now.'

'Do any of these make you think who they might be from?'

Ciara stared at the messages. Her face was pale, her mouth slack, her green eyes bloodshot. It was as if she had moved through grief to a place where there was no feeling anymore, just a sleepless exhaustion. 'That one.' She tapped the line "you know they talk about you because they're jealous".

'That sounds like Harley.'

'You think these messages are from her.'

'No. This is clearly a lover.' She pointed at "I can still smell you on myself". 'This is not something Harley would say to anyone. Not even a lover.' She snorted. 'Even the part about the twist isn't her. It's too encouraging.'

'So who?'

Ciara shrugged. Boris, finally free of the Lakeside Roosters, joined them.

'Bourbon, Ciara?'

Her face lit up. She looked years younger. 'Thank you Boris. Please.'

Her eyes followed him as he poured the drink. Catherine tried to stifle a smile, then realised that she could yodel and Ciara wouldn't look away from Boris.

'What about "You've hurt me once too often"? Does that ring any bells for you?'

'Ring any bells?'

'Does it make you think of anyone?'

Ciara chewed her lip. 'It's the kind of power trip Harley does, but not her words. I think this might be a person not connected to the circus. Another who knew her would have heard her speak of overthinking the twist. We all do such things.'

Ciara went back to admiring Boris.

Catherine followed her gaze. 'Yep, that's his second best pair of jeans, looks like he might have washed them this month too.'

Ciara gave her a quizzical look. 'Why do you say that?'

'You can tell when he hasn't by the way they bunch around his ankles.' This was met with silence, so she went on. 'Because I'm trying to understand who sent these texts and you seem more interested in my hired muscle.'

Boris joined them, passing Ciara's drink. 'I thought I was the brains.'

'I'm glad someone does, dear.'

Ciara raised her glass and sparrow sipped. Boris had found a swizzle stick from somewhere; not a standard Glasgow Palace drinking accessory.

'Do you know who it might be?' Boris prompted.

Ciara smiled, only for him. 'Some of it sounds like Harley, but too much does not. None of it sounds like Virginia.'

Boris sighed. One of the footy players was returning to the bar. 'Oh well, we keep going then.'

Catherine took a long moment. 'He's a good man.'

'I can tell.'

Catherine kept her gaze steadily on Ciara, who was looking towards the window. 'He will do anything for anyone.'

Ciara slowly turned to grin at Catherine. 'The best people will. Do you mind that I've noticed too?'

Catherine took a sip, bigger than she meant to. 'I'm glad someone else has, that's all.' Her stomach had the empty feeling that came with fasting or cowardice. Suddenly keen to change the subject, she said, 'Do you know Silver's father?'

Her lip curled. 'He is a stupid man.'

'He's in town.'

'Of course he is.'

'Do you know him?'

'I have never met him, but I know him. Because I knew her. You can see how a person has been treated by their father when you live with them. He was horrid to her. She is an ornament. He is one of those family men who say they love family, but they only love themselves.'

'He's asking me to look into the matter for him.'

'So he trusts you. Does that mean you have to trust him?'

Catherine shook her head, hoping the matter of trust wouldn't be too finely explored.

'Good.' Ciara stared ahead. 'Stupid man.'

'So, just to be clear. You haven't been in touch with the others in the troupe, aside from Jean, right?'

'Yes, Jean called.' Ciara's faraway expression got no nearer. 'I have texted three of the others. I got very polite responses. I think they are all against me.'

'I'd have thought you'd all come together.'

'They are. They all met at Ginia's place yesterday.'

'How do you know?'

'Harley posted pictures. She knew I would see them.'

The pang in Catherine's stomach returned; she hadn't noticed it go. Sometimes Catherine hated people.

'So Harley's partying with the troupe. I guess that means whatever was worrying her about the phone has gone away. That's good news for Boris.'

'I wouldn't be so sure. She pretends to forget things, just so it hurts more when she pounces.' Ciara spoke with a lightness that often came with talking about trauma. When the desire to brush off heavy things affected the way people spoke about them. Lying to themselves by use of tonality.

'What happens now?' Ciara asked after a minute.

'We find out what else is on the phone, we keep looking for other things. I'll talk to Virginia about the mood of the troupe. Keep in mind that now the police are also investigating. I'll get Jean's number off you, if you don't mind. She sounds like a good place to start.'

Ciara grimaced. 'So we wait for someone to get arrested. Maybe me.'

'Why would you say that?'

There was a hint of moisture in her eyes. 'When I think of what Harley can do. I wonder if she would make the girls remember things.'

'Maybe Silver's death really was just an accident.'

'That would be strange. That wasn't the hard part of the routine.'

Catherine leaned in, closely watching Ciara's face as she spoke. 'Could it be suicide?'

Ciara's eyes closed hard. 'No. She wouldn't do that to the show. That would be even more horrible than the reality.'

'Which is?'

'That she's gone.' Ciara leaned forward as she said it. Catherine knew how tired that kind of sentence could make you.

'You should try to eat something.'

'I don't feel like it.'

Catherine stood, lay a hand on the woman's shoulder and murmured in her ear, 'Your feelings are overriding your survival senses, but it'll make the feelings worse. I'll order some chips. You don't have to eat many of them to get your caloric intake right up there with Boris.'

Boris sat down bodily with a plate of said chips plus a Parma and glass of soda water.

'It is your break?' Ciara asked. Boris nodded, offering her a chip.

She took one. 'Boris. I want to go. Will you walk me to the train?'

Behind Ciara, Catherine supressed her exasperated grin.

'Ahm. Sure.' Boris put two chips in his mouth and stood again. Catherine could see his legs were aching. It was in the small wince as he got off the stool.

'Will you come, Catherine?'

She flashed him a winning look. 'I want to keep thinking here. You keep Ciara safe.' Her ghost of a wink reminded him that he was on the clock.

'You just want to eat my dinner.'

'Everything tastes better when it's seasoned by your efforts.'

The air blew cold on them the moment they were outside. Boris tried to savour the taste of the chips in his mouth. That failed, so he just sent a hard stare in the vague direction of Antarctica. Ciara leaned into him, and he put an arm around her. There was a swish as his puffer jacket slid against hers. Her fingers came down hard on his shoulder and his whole forehead creased, not only because different parts of his face were cold. At first he thought she was trying to scare him, then he recognised she was afraid.

He looked at her face as she stared at the pavement. 'You will get through this.'

Her face flickered. She started walking. 'I will get through everything. I just won't enjoy it.'

Boris paced beside her, wondering what to say. He decided to go with honesty. 'What are you afraid of?'

She spoke almost immediately. 'I worry. They will either silence me or frame me.'

'Did they always hate you?'

They stepped out three more paces before she answered. 'No. I was accepted, but still different. Now something awful has happened.' She paused. 'I think this is how people are, Boris.'

He blinked. There was a pinch of rain in the air. 'I like to think differently.'

'I know.' She squeezed his arm.

'Catherine will find out what happened. It's what she does.'

Ciara nodded. 'Maybe even if she found the truth, it wouldn't be enough for people. I think my career is done here.'

'Why?'

'I told Catherine, the whole troupe were at Ginia's house last night. I was not invited. They have decided it was me.'

'Do you really know that?'

Her voice pitched against the air. 'Why wouldn't they invite me if not?'

He stopped. She stopped. 'Because Harley suspects you were there with me in the park,' said Boris. 'Because she thinks we have the phone, which we do.' He watched as she brushed rain off her eyes. He had hardly noticed. 'Because people are mean, and sometimes follow bullies. It doesn't mean you did it, or even that anyone thinks it, it just becomes what happened.'

The kiss took him totally by surprise. Her tongue was so warm it seemed to come from a different planet.

Catherine caught Boris' eye as he came back into the pub. His cheeks were flushed and he tried to hide a smile. Smiles shouldn't exist in a week of death in a cold climate.

He moved quickly to his place at the bar and didn't even look at his parma. There was only one explanation.

'Did you just get a pash?'

Boris looked at his feet. 'I didn't start it.'

'Jesus, Boris. We're investigating who killed her friend. I'm starting to think it might even be her.'

Boris didn't make eye contact, but his gestures were apologetic. 'I know. Not cool. I didn't mean to. It just happened.'

'Do you even want this parma?'

He checked his watch. 'Oh yeah, I have five more minutes' break.'

'You can get me a wine, anyway.'

Boris made himself busy, chewing his mouth slightly as he did so.

'So do you think she's full of it entirely because she kissed me or because she didn't seem at all interested in you?'

'I'm hardly so shallow. Besides, she's the second girl today interested in you. The winter is clearly making people lower their standards.'

'Agree to disagree.'

'On the dropped standards?'

He passed her a glass of shiraz. 'On you being shallow.'

Catherine took a long sip. The bar was almost empty. Even Stevie had stumbled out, usually a sign that Catherine would have to leave in a few rounds. 'Her interest was lacklustre at best.'

Boris gave a small smile. 'On the contrary.'

'I mean to the case, Boris.'

He grinned at the glass he was wiping. 'I know, but a bloke has to take his fun.'

'More professional if you didn't.'

'Unfair.' He put the glass back in the rack. 'I don't remember giving you a hard time when a certain client got handsy.'

'That was different.'

'He almost stabbed you.'

'Different.' Her voice rose.

'He almost stabbed *me*.'

'Different.' Catherine emphasised each syllable, though it sounded weak even to her.

Boris slowly raised two hands. 'Because Ciara hasn't stabbed anyone.'

'My experience of romance ceased entirely even before he started stabbing people.' Catherine was suddenly very aware of the small scar near Boris' eyebrow. 'Well, before I knew he was stabbing people.' She dismissed the premise with a fencer's flourish. 'Okay, point well made. Stick it where you like, but be aware of the risks.'

Boris checked the chip packets for stocktake. 'Two women in a day. I like them both. It's not fair.'

'I'm here arguing with you while my bed lies cold as ice, unless Minty's on it. Cry me the mother truckin' Nile, buddy.'

Boris called from the storage cupboard. 'My bed's cold too, aside from when my housemate's dog is there.'

'How is Buttons?'

'Still flatulent.'

'Good,' she said quietly.

Boris returned, armfuls of crinkle cut against his chest. 'You are so petulant when you lose an argument.'

'I didn't lose an argument. I think she's full of it. Why would you blank at a major piece of potential evidence?' She flicked at the message printout in front of her.

'Maybe she's tired after four days of wondering who's gonna get her, Harley's goons or the cops. All the while her colleagues are consoling each other behind her back. People are mean.'

Catherine tried not to say it, but it was too late. 'And if people are mean, isn't it just great we have brave knights like you to protect us?

Boris was quick, and quiet. 'And smart people to tell us the world is just fine.'

Boris walked Catherine home mostly in silence. Neither discussed a nightcap. Afterwards, Boris hurried home along the train line. The street was deserted. For a Saturday night, this was unheard of, but understandable in the chill. Boris started calculating the hours until spring, but gave up and just licked his lips. He couldn't taste ice, or Ciara. He grunted, thinking about Catherine's snide dismissal of her. The well-rehearsed Boris/Catherine shtick of him being inferior only hurt when it was apparent she believed it.

A bat flapped above, and all thought left him aside from fight and flight. His knees bent and his hands rose to hip-level, ready to strike but not threatening. After thirty seconds, there was no further sound aside from the glide of a tram a hundred metres away. Boris thought of Catherine safe in her flat, while he walked home scared because he had made himself a target to save her.

'Check yourself, Shakhovskoy,' he muttered. He'd done that deliberately. And, he knew, women felt this fear all the time. This was a bad day for him, but for most women, this was a fact of the night. He muttered a small apology on behalf of all his gender and walked on.

He moved away from the train line bike path, using a different route to the previous two nights. He saw two men walking a large dog. Boris crossed the road. They didn't look at him. One of them walked with a limp.

Boris watched them go past. He couldn't catch many words, but was sure he heard something about an A minor, which didn't seem threatening. He paused ten metres later and tied his shoe, listening for footsteps. Nothing. He turned and checked; they were almost at the next corner. Boris blew on fingers that were almost numb with cold.

Almost one hundred and fifty metres to home. Officially in sprinting range. No one around. No nefarious action for almost three days. Was he still overreacting?

He could take the alley through to his street or do the block. The dim white glow of the street lamps gave only a sense of protection. Boris took a deep breath and moved into the alley. It had worked the previous night. Even in the dark he could see his breath in front of him. He moved quickly, his legs pushing. He remembered walking through his childhood house in the night, afraid of ghosts and wanting the sanctuary of his bed.

Nothing came out of the darkness to greet him. The glow of his own street grew closer. He emerged. One woman walked away from him on the other side of the street. Boris took out his keys, walked the last bit with them in his hand, ready to strike.

He walked up his path to the side door. He turned and took a last look.

Just when his lungs prepared to breathe out a final gasp of relief, he saw it. The red glow of a cigarette. In the block over the road. The house that had been seemingly half built for months. Someone was there. Smoking a cigarette. Why would anyone be over there tonight?

In the cold. Late at night. Across the road from his house. Too cold even for teenagers on a Saturday night.

Boris could only think of one reason.

He double bolted the door. Checked the windows. Heard the television in both his housemates' rooms. He took a beer to his own room, and even though he told himself not to, he hid under the covers. Just for a little while. Touching his face where it had been hurt. Feeling completely helpless.

10

Success is measured in wealth and love. They are intertwined. They are everything.
~Anthony Barwick

Catherine awoke annoyed. It hit before she knew her name, what species she was, or that red wine was actually a slow release poison. There was just a twist in her abdomen that knew she had a problem to solve and knew she didn't like it.

The pain in her shoulder had some volume in the morning. It was better than yesterday, but still there.

She pulled apart the pale drapes of her lounge room and started stocktaking her worries.

The blue hat was a carbon copy of six others with different ribbon.

Australia could never be progressive while it was so comfortable.

This winter would go on forever. Antarctica was an angry continent, abandoned as the Gondwana supercontinent, that would punish the world, Australia first.

As a self-employed milliner with rich parents, she was the problem with comfortable Australia. Here she was. Tired, hungover, and nowhere near uncomfortable enough to do anything about it.

Boris was being played and he liked it.

Humans aren't built to be comfortable, hence the widespread anxiety and wilful ignoring of nature right across the middle and upper classes.

All those issues irked Catherine. But only one had plucked the tension in her like a harp string.

Bloody Boris.

For the right cause, even the wrong cause, but one that needed him, he would walk into fire. He wouldn't even think, that was the problem. He wouldn't even think.

Of course it was the best thing about him, unless it was going against you. Of course he did want things for himself, mostly food and drink, but that was all hidden under various layers of wanting to please and protect others, so that even he didn't know what he wanted.

She looked at her phone beside the couch, where Boris usually sat.

This was the kind of thing she liked to discuss with Boris. Of course she did.

Was she jealous? No.

A realisation punched her and she flinched. She was watching him about to be hurt by someone else. It showed her how cruel it was. Even when he was getting hurt for her.

He's such a fucking idiot.

Boris woke to the smell of an animal on top of him. The animal was sleeping, and domesticated, and certainly not a bald thug, so he just rolled over and snuffled into the pillow with the ease of a lazy man on Sunday. Sometimes you can fit into your day just like a pet can fit into the fold of your body. His head knew terror as he dozed, but his body knew nothing of it. That's the thing with bodies. They can shed a great deal of feeling. It's useful in a life full of danger.

He was about to fall asleep when the thought of Ciara and Jolene came to him almost simultaneously. Pleasure and guilt washed over him in a warm and almost welcome flow. Then Catherine entered his mind and it all was tinged with a righteous resentment.

The dog farted and Boris knew, day of rest or not, it was time to rise and greet whatever today had to throw at him. Derring do, derring don't, or whatever.

He inched to the window and looked out. Grey light pierced the room and he blinked twice. Must be about nine. Not much traffic, not that this was ever a main street. The house across the road looked like a harmless site, with no work done on a Sunday. Boris decided it was time to get aggressive. Or at least less cowardly. Daylight was weak in winter, but it took away the darkness and there was less to be scared of. He moved to go downstairs. Turning to see if the dog would follow him.

'Buttons?'

The dog slept on. He made it look easy.

Arsehole. Not a care in the bloody world.

At least he felt fresher than most Sundays. He wondered what Catherine was doing. In usual circumstances, they would have breakfast, but today didn't seem to be the day. This knight could get his own.

He had a date with Jolene, if he wasn't bashed to death in the next eight hours. The thought gave him pause. Maybe he should cancel. No.

Ciara had kissed him, though he hadn't instigated anything.

He put a pod in the new coffee machine his housemate had bought and thought about the environment again. Looking out in the back yard, he saw seven recycled pod wind structures and about six hours' worth of junk moving and weeding that no one would get around to until the next inspection. Even the deck chairs up at the back were surrounded by self-sown spring onions, garlic flowers, and various other weeds that Boris was pretty sure you couldn't eat.

The first coffee didn't hit the sides. But he was impatient to find the evidence of him being watched, using the bravery of daylight. He jammed another pod in the machine, filled his cup, took it outside, and wondered why his legs were suddenly cold. He realised at the open door that he was only in a dressing gown.

Two minutes later he was in yesterday's jeans and his green puffer jacket, and his coffee was already tepid. He strode over the road, searching the timber frames and flapping insulation paper to see if anyone was around. He saw no one. The fencing to the building site was intact, not that he expected a meathead-size hole blown out of it.

Inside the building site, he moved slowly towards where he had seen the cigarette glow. He could see where the person, probably a man, possibly Harley had been. It was where – in three months' time – the back door of one the units would be. He slowed. The footprints were mostly male, or at least large, working boots, which made Boris think of steel caps and wish that he had some. There was only one set of prints. So only one person had been there since the last rain. Yesterday afternoon. The place was well maintained. Little rubbish. Few offcuts. A wooden box at the front of the site held all the rubbish.

He walked slowly backwards. Other footprints were visible in the next unit, but he wanted to check thoroughly. He tried to make his eyes soft, the way Catherine always talked about. He didn't have to move far. At the front door of the second unit he found another set of footprints, like someone had been dancing wildly. There were also a half dozen cigarette butts, and a seven-centimetre length of silver, glittery ribbon.

Boris stared at it. It was like finding a dolphin in a wheat field. He was completely perplexed. A raven squawked an expletive. It didn't help him.

'What the actual–?'

When you carry the weight of an annoyance in your gut, you should never try to make a hat. Resentment can bring change into society, and pain to all concerned, but it doesn't make good art. Pain can bring great art. Love, hate, grief. Resentment will only hollow out the artist while their fingers do something badly.

Unless you can let go of the rest of the world, there is no way to make something that is either beautiful or functional. Catherine was ignoring the clock, because the clock would indicate how much time she had wasted in that headspace.

Of course, when you're feeling the way she was, there was no way she was going to not try. She knew her failings, and the fact that she always tried too hard was one she actually liked.

So she kept trying to decorate the blue monstrosity in front of her, even though she knew that it wouldn't happen today. It wasn't so much that the hat was bad, but that it wasn't good. It was perfectly average, a missed opportunity for style to progress in a rather striking shade of royal blue. Catherine pushed a new angle. Her fingers, which sometimes felt like those of a god, felt like a platypus claws, sheathed in gloves, and about as useful when it came to millinery. Perhaps this could be the platypus of hats, she thought, letting her eyes fog. Perhaps this could be the thing nature threw up, just to mess with everyone.

Or it could just be crap.

She sighed and considered donning another pair of socks. She already had two on and her feet still felt like they could fall off any second. There was an Ugg boot outlet across the road, but they weren't open on

Sundays. Catherine had vowed not to get another pair, as her last pair was given to her by her mother, and such things couldn't be tolerated.

Dopamine hit with the vibrating of her phone. Boris. Catherine regarded it for a full eight seconds, wondering if she wanted to hear his voice.

She picked up. 'Save me from mediocrity.'

He sniffed. 'Hmm.'

'Can't a girl try jaunty every now and again?'

'I can tell when it's forced. And I'm annoyed at you too.'

'It's not my fault that you're an idiot.' She said it louder than she meant to.

'And not mine that you're a haughty, arrogant know-all.'

Catherine's tone fell to the temperature of her feet. 'Did that sound as good as you planned?'

'Yes, actually.'

'What do you need, Boris?'

'Sadly, I need you. Someone was watching me last night. They were watching from the house over the road. Now I'm checking it out and I can't make head nor tail of what I'm looking at. So I need a smart haughty friend.' There was a pause. 'I'm not happy about it either.'

Catherine took a deep breath. 'Okay. Sorry you were followed. How do you know they're not watching you now?'

'I hadn't thought of that. See how much I need you?'

'I'll be eight minutes.' She hung up. Grimaced. Smiled. And got annoyed at herself for smiling. Honestly: men.

'One doesn't surveil while dancing, usually.'

'And yet.'

Catherine looked at the footprints. They definitely gave the impression of a sort of shuffle. Combine that with the cigarette butts, and you had the view that someone had had themselves a small disco, in a very contained space, across the road from Boris' house on a Saturday night.

'I have a thought.' Boris turned from scanning the street for assailants.

'What's that?'

'It's not helpful. It goes: what the actual fuck?'

Boris came back and re-examined the footprints. They were heavier than his, so this person was upwards of 90kg. He looked at the piece of ribbon in Catherine's hand and swore.

Catherine looked at him sharply. 'What?'

'Do you remember what Harley's speciality in circus was?'

'Hula hoops. But what's that got to do with–?' She looked back at the ribbon. 'Oh. My. Goodness.'

'These aren't Harley's footprints.'

The pattern made sense. 'No, someone much heavier. Who seemed to pass the time smoking and hula hooping.'

Boris pinched the bridge of his nose. 'That should make me feel less threatened, and yet.'

'At least it wasn't a fire breather.'

'At least it wasn't a lion tamer.'

Catherine rolled her eyes. 'Oh please Boris, it's the 21st century.'

'Oh of course, no one has claw mark scars on their back these days.'

'Ancient history Boris, and that wasn't my fault.'

Boris said something unintelligible. Catherine was grateful her phone rang, which meant she could ignore him.

'This is Catherine.'

'Catherine. Barwick here. What's new?'

'Nothing too exciting, Mr Barwick. We're still trying to decipher the messages on the phone.'

'I haven't been able to make anything of them.'

Catherine blinked. She didn't expect him to be able to since he hadn't seen his daughter in years. Yet some people always needed to feel part of the team. 'We'll keep working on it.'

'I'm just not confident of a result unless we push.'

'Just to be clear, what's a result in this instance? An arrest?'

There was a pause. Too long. 'Just the truth, Catherine. I just want a true sense of things to be out there.'

Catherine watched Boris, who made a face that told her she was scowling. 'We'll keep you posted. Pushing is what we do.'

'I'm counting on it.'

As she rang off, Catherine was aware of feeling three times as cold as she had a moment before. She sat on the concrete slab of what would one day be one of a series of three units. Even without the other slabs, the view wouldn't be great.

'Boris.'

'Yeah.'

'I'm sorry I was dismissive of you. Can we have different opinions on Ciara and just see what happens?'

Boris sat by her. 'Are you okay?'

She breathed out slowly. Her breath was visible in the cold. Boris thought he saw a ghost of a tear in her eye. 'I will be, but just right now I feel like everyone has an ulterior motive in this. And suddenly I need you.'

He put an arm around her. 'Okay. What's next then?'

She leaned into him. Just for a moment. Feeling his bulk and just for a second, warm.

'Barwick. He's full of shit, we knew, but let's find out more about him.'

'Neal?'

'Exactly.'

Fifteen minutes later, Boris was blowing some feeling back into his fingers, having dinked a ride to Neal's on Catherine's Vespa. While Catherine had her own gloves, Boris had insisted 'he'd be fine' as it was only an eight minute commute. Eight minutes is a long time, especially when you're a nervous motorbike passenger and temperature is going into the impressive minus. The grey skies had spelled a Cormac McCarthy-esque doom for him as he tried to grip Catherine's coat with whatever strength he had left.

All self-pity left him as June opened the door. Fatigue had turned the rims of her eyes almost charcoal against her brown skin.

'Catherine, hello my dear.'

'Oh June, you look–' She couldn't go on.

June smiled ruefully. 'Yes, I am aware. I'm afraid I feel even worse.'

'I'm so sorry.'

'It will be worth it to meet this young being.' She patted her occupied belly and turned – precariously, Catherine thought – down the hallway.

'The cheerful idiot I married is out in his shed. Does he know you're coming?'

'No,' Catherine lied, deciding to take on any matrimonial resentment for Neal. It was the least she could do. 'We're being bad mannered for a righteous cause.'

'I never had any doubts, my dear.' June flopped on the red couch with a sound that was two parts pain and three parts resignation.

Catherine and Boris went quickly through the back door, knowing they were likely pushing the single heating system to its limit even with a ten second opening.

Neal, by comparison, looked utterly delighted as they walked through the door. 'Sorry to barge in on a Sunday,' Boris remarked.

'Not at all, dear sir, I'm getting ahead on my work so I can take some time when the young one arrives. Plus I have some rather interesting news of my own.' Neal gestured to the chairs, one on the opposite side of his desk, which Boris took.

'Really?' Catherine flopped into the strange green and blue armchair that adorned one corner of Neal's office. 'You're an amazing person to visit on a cold day.'

'Well thank you. I'm still running one more diagnostic, but it's almost certain that your phone hasn't been in use for longer than seventeen days.'

'Seventeen days isn't long.'

'And there's not much use on it,'

'So maybe "You've hurt me once too often" is a conversation continued from another burner?'

'How many phones did she need? She was an acrobat, right?'

Catherine stared at the phone, as if daring it to give more information. 'An acrobat that used drugs and was estranged from her entire family, according to her dad. Maybe she dabbled in something else. Maybe she was in touch with her siblings. Acrobats don't make much money, and as far as we know she didn't have a day job.'

Neal looked at the photo of his parents on the east wall. 'Family money perhaps?'

'She inherited some serious coin. But trips to New York aren't cheap.' Catherine waved a hand languidly at Neal. 'It's the family I want to find out about. Anthony Barwick is the name of Silver's father. He tried to hire me, which I let him do, then he tried to hit Boris, which he failed at. He's a loose cannon and I suspect he's up to his neck in something.'

'You don't think he had something to do with the murder?'

'I'm not convinced it's a murder, but I'm convinced something happened. And he's no angel. Nor is he that smart, so I'm keen to learn more about him.'

'Anthony Barwick.' Neal wrote it down.

'The business is Barwick Steel and Holdings. See what you can find,'

'Are you in a hurry?'

'I'm not. Boris?'

'I have a date in four hours, and I really should shower beforehand.'

Neal gave his most beatific smile. 'You're evolving Boris, no question.'

'Don't you start.'

'Of course, you did start from such a way beh–'

'Oi.'

Neal's grin flashed again. 'Oh Boris, I apologise. I would blame Catherine but it's unfair. Maybe I'm just getting my last teasing out before I become a father''

Boris softened. 'My Dad teased me all the time.'

Outside, there was a flash of lightning.

Neal's eyes were drawn again to his parents' photo. 'Then perhaps it's you? Do you think you know you're special, and invite teasing so we don't hate you for it?'

Boris swivelled the chair back and forth. 'Neal, I really don't think–'

'If everyone teases you, and loves you, is teasing a problem?'

'Well, I learned to laugh at myself.'

Catherine's smiled, enjoying her friend's moment. 'Mr Barwick strikes me as a man who can't do that. I suspect it's at the heart of his tragedy.'

'Nah, I think the heart of it is his daughter died at twenty three having left his family.'

'Nice downer, Boris.'

'I'm here to help.'

Neal interrupted. 'I'll be able to tell you more later. But I can say that Barwick Holdings has not been the business name for twenty years. In fact, I have brought up quite a list of potential past names.'

'Phoenix companies?'

'That's what I'm thinking.'

Boris shifted in the chair. 'Are you two speaking Gryffindor now?'

Neal grinned. 'I'm Hufflepuff all the way, same as you Boris. A phoenix company is when you declare bankruptcy and then when the debts are gone, start a new company with a different name. In this case, he can't go past his own name. I'm sure he has a great relationship with ASIC.'

'Oh, you can do that in business? If I don't pay my debts, I can't get beer.'

'So good that alcohol is keeping you on the straight and narrow. My Sikh ancestors would never have seen that coming. Now, you can watch me work, but it won't get you anything further. Oh, hang on.' He peered at his screen. 'Confirmed. It's only 17 days old, I'm certain of it.'

'Curiouser and curiouser,' mumbled Catherine.

'Catherine,' his voice was sombre. 'I think your time has been wasted with this. All the messages seem to have come in at the same time, as well that the first one you saw, the "everything you need", which is now visible.'

'When?'

'It's corrupted, so I know it's sometime in the past 17 days, but I don't know when.'

'Does this mean that last message may also be corrupted?'

'It's possible. Unless you can see a pattern that I can't, I think this has been a dead end.'

Catherine sighed. 'Bugger, sorry Neal.'

'Always nice to see you both, but there's no answers here.'

Neal handed her the phone. She stared at it briefly before putting it in her bag, feeling the emptiness in her gut that always came with wasted time, even after a big breakfast. As they walked out, Neal called to them, 'Oh, would you mind going around the side? I suspect, and hope, that June is having a nap.'

Thunder rolled.

'So what's your date today?' Catherine asked Boris, trying to lighten her mood. 'A walk in the Treasury Gardens?'

'I thought perhaps croquet.'

Catherine got home at 2pm to find a familiar grey BMW parked outside her house. If Virginia had brought champagne, it would be almost acceptable. Though the look on her friend's face as she stepped out of the car told her otherwise.

'Hello, dear.'

'Catherine. I'm sorry. I just need to talk it through again. The police want to know about everyone's supplements. Like I have a clue about that.'

'Let's go upstairs.'

A few minutes later, two teas were rapidly cooling on Catherine's coffee table in the grey light that swamped the lounge room. Catherine was watching Virginia desperately trying to make Minty sit on her. The Russian Blue wanted exactly none of it and Catherine wondered how her pet had become a better judge of character than she was.

'I don't know what they're getting at. All the girls have different needs and desires. Harley always wants more muscle density and so is on a keto/high protein diet. Jean swears by her cupping technique that she gets every week and all of them have some form of herbal supplements or others. It's all horrible teas and micro doses of whatever.'

'Do you know what Silver used?'

'She was mostly a tea person, ginseng mostly. Your man found her stuff. It was horrid. She drank it all the time. One of those instances where it had to be good for you, as it was so awful to smell. God knows what it tasted like.' Virginia's face was screwed up at the memory.

'Would she use it before performances?'

'She would use it all the time. I think she was taking it six times a day.'

'Did they examine the jar that Boris found?'

'Who?'

'The police.'

'Oh yes. They took all her locker stuff away, after the report came back.' Virginia looked out the window.

Catherine was uncomfortable about her afternoon being eaten up by watching this woman cry again. Part of her felt heartless; the other half was just rolling her eyes.

She shifted her position on the couch, becoming square on with Virginia. 'Why did you have all the troupe to your house but not Ciara?'

Virginia blinked rapidly. 'How–?'

'Ciara noticed. I don't know how. But she came to us afterwards.'

'Oh, God.' Virginia doubled over on the couch. When she came up her lips were moving as if she were saying a quiet prayer. 'Harley didn't want her there. I thought it was wrong, but I also didn't want to upset the women any more than they were. Plus, Jean wasn't there either.'

'You didn't question why Harley didn't want her there?'

'I knew exactly why she didn't want her there. Harley is certain that Ciara did something to Silver that caused the accident. I think it's nonsense and I pushed the unity agenda very hard at the gathering.'

'That Ciara wasn't invited to.' Catherine didn't mean to sound quite so pointed, but the memories of a thousand vulnerable afternoons at school had come back to her in a flood.

'I was just trying to support everyone. I'm sure that once the police finalise the investigation all will be well. The WorkSafe people seemed satisfied. They were very reasonable.'

Catherine tried to mask her feelings by sipping tea. Perhaps she should have poured a gin. 'Then why are you so scared?'

'Because what if they decide it was me? Or if it was my fault.' She leaned forward again, clutching her stomach. 'I'll never. I'll be. Oh God. I already have parents taking their kids out of the school.'

'How stable is the circus, financially?'

Virginia frowned. 'That's not a thing I discuss lightly, Catherine.'

'It's not something I ask lightly. I'm trying to see all the moving pieces. How stable are you, where does the money come from? The troupe or the school?'

Virginia exhaled. 'The troupe makes its money back with each show, but it doesn't make profit. The school makes some profit and that's what keeps us running, though on occasion I have made a donation from my own funds. Most of the troupe teach at the school.'

'Your own funds?'

'Catherine, like you, I have been fortunate enough to be born with some money. We have to give back, don't you agree?'

Such talk always made Catherine want to reach for the cyanide – not the content, but the assumed superiority. She changed the topic. 'Who doesn't work for you at the school?'

'Ciara. She works in a café in town. And Silver didn't either.'

'What did Silver do for money?'

'She seems… Seemed to be independently wealthy. Inherited some cash and was clever with it. Investments and such. She didn't like to talk about it. It put a wedge between her and the others. They're a tight-knit group.'

Catherine prepared to burst a bubble. 'It still seems strange to me that you say that. All I've heard during my investigation is how dominating Harley is.'

Virginia gesticulated broadly. 'She's a big personality. And she is exquisitely talented. You should see what she can do with the hulas. She's a master.'

'Good with people, too.' It wasn't a question.

'Have you spoken to anyone aside from Ciara about her?'

'Just you and her, but it's on my list for today.'

'Oh.' Virginia took a deep breath. 'I am sorry I didn't put my foot down about inviting Ciara. I didn't realise she would find out.'

'I think Harley made sure she did.'

'Oh god. How awful. I will call her. I will. I can't have her angry.'

'Angry? What about supported?'

'Oh, of course. It's just. Well. I've only seen Ciara angry once. One of the parents at the school accused her of leading him on. She was so angry she punched through a car window – not his, another parent. I just couldn't believe the amount of rage she keeps in her. It's why she doesn't teach anymore. God only knows what she might do if I don't call.'

Catherine leaned in. 'What happened?'

'She ran away with a bleeding hand. I paid for the car window. We lost both families, the parent who accused her and the poor woman whose car was smashed. But it blew over. Everything does, you see?'

Catherine didn't even ask about Ciara's hand. 'I think Silver would disagree.'

'Well of course. This is something much more…' she struggled to find the word, 'different.'

'Ok. Virginia. I have to work, I'm pursuing several leads. I'll let you know what bears fruit.'

Virginia took the hint. Leaving her tepid tea on the table, she took herself out. Catherine closed the door and listened to her heels clicking down the stairs to the street. On the other side of the lounge room, Minty was cleaning her backside.

Catherine flopped on the couch and thought about bravery. Small bravery and large, it all came down to what you valued. All aspects of how Virginia ran her troupe spoke of cowardice to her. Weeks earlier, Catherine had thought Virginia was a fearless woman who championed feminism and circus. Now it seemed all she wanted was not to offend anyone, or at least not be caught doing it.

Unbidden, Catherine knew what she needed to do with the blue hat. She sniffed, went to the bedroom to put on two more jumpers, then went downstairs to her workshop. She could work on two problems at once. She was born for it.

Two hours later, Boris was thinking about Ciara and Jolene and wondering when he'd become someone that thought about two women at the same time. Usually, one woman in his life was enough to keep him hopeless for hours. Now suddenly he was going on a date with a woman he liked after kissing another woman he liked the night before.

It didn't feel right, at all. Catherine had talked him through dating in the twenty first century and he knew people did this all the time; he just wasn't people, not like that. He looked at himself in the mirror.

Okay. Number one, she kissed you, you didn't start anything. Number two, Jolene will probably come to her senses and not show up. Number three.

He struggled on number three.

Number three, I want to go, so even if it makes me an arsehole, I'm going.

He walked out of his building and saw the bald man straight away.

Suddenly all thought of what chivalry meant in a modern world seemed ridiculous.

Baldy wore no jacket today, but was just as menacing in trackies. He looked like he could fight, and he wasn't hiding. He stood in front of the building site.

Boris, in his best shirt and smelling just faintly, faintly of eau de toilette felt his mouth go dry.

'She wants what you took.' The man's voice was deep, gruff, and suited his rough head perfectly.

'I could take you a lot more seriously if you had your hula hoop.' Boris started down the street.

The footsteps came quickly.

Boris turned and swung, collecting the man's neck with just a glance. The thug took two steps back quickly. Boris followed and moved his left foot between the man's legs, pushing him down, while grabbing his hoodie so he went down slow. The thug snapped his right arm across Boris's wrists, but Boris was already letting go. Baldy fell the last ten centimetres quickly.

'I don't want to hurt you.'

Baldy was up quickly, an athlete's recovery. 'You won't.' He swung, Boris ducked and jabbed at his chest, half connecting. A yell came from across the road. Three kids about ten, all long hair and baseball caps, were pointing and shouting. Mostly noise, but Boris could make out one line. 'Leave him alone, dickhead.'

'Call the police,' Boris called back.

The kid's eyes widened as he changed his view on who was attacking whom. Boris let him go, splayed his hands, looking at the bald man.

'Hear that curly? The cavalry's coming.'

'They can get the phone off you.'

Boris's hands went wide. 'They'd struggle. I don't have it.'

'I reckon you know where it is. We won't go away until we've got it. You'll see me again.' He walked away. 'The circus is coming to town, buddy.'

The kids called out. 'Yeah, keep on walking.' 'Walk away.' And 'Shut up, Toby.' Showing the full gamut of bravado and caution. Baldy shot them a look and kept going.

Boris sucked his knuckles, wondering if anything had been achieved. He seemed to have won the round, and between that and some assumptions about hula hoopers, he felt less scared than he had for days. His stomach turned as he realised the bloke would be back and would bring a mate next time. Boris thought of his own mates: Catherine, Andy, Neal. None of them great brawlers. He blew out a long stream of breath.

'You all right?'

The kids were close by. One was walking a small dog whose tail was doing overtime.

'Yeah. Thanks. Did you call the cops?'

'I don't have a phone. I'm ten.'

'Oh right. That was brave of you then.'

The kids smiled. One asked, 'Do you owe him money?'

'Nah.' The thug was out of sight now. 'I don't even know his name.'

'I called the wrong guy a dickhead then.'

Boris grinned. 'I'm not so sure about that mate.' He checked his watch. He was sweating, but had no time to shower. He walked to the tram stop, feeling his heartbeat starting to slow. Even if the date did start with Jolene standing him up, the day would be improving.

11

They couldn't fly unless I gave them a sky.
~Virginia Baillieu

Boris' date, in fact, started with a beer. Boris walked into the Brunswick Green at three minutes to five and Jolene was waiting with two fresh pints and a crossword under her pen.

'Hey.'

'Hey.' She kissed his cheek and something flipped in his head. He blinked, repeatedly.

'I hope you don't mind. I just assumed you were a lager man.'

'I don't mind and I am. How did you guess?'

'It was either that, or you would be completely offended by that. You might have been the homebrew, microbrewery type that hated lager.'

'So it was a risk.'

She tapped the glass of her own pint thoughtfully. 'I didn't really see it as scary until I bought it.'

Boris smiled. 'Even if you'd bought a dry sherry, it would still be a nice thought.'

'That's how I calmed myself down. I figured you'd be polite even if I was wrong. Also, if you were going to get mean about something small it wouldn't be worth staying for a second beer.'

Boris, who could still taste adrenaline after the fight, was conscious of drinking too quickly. He put the pint on the table and looked at Jolene, exceedingly pleased that the prospect of a second beer was in the air.

'I like your hair.'

'Thanks.' She ran a hand through her thick, dark locks. She had a shaved undercut, yet it was more understated than most of the equivalent fashions in the bar. 'A bit different to my overalls at the garage.'

'Tell me how you got into cars?'

'It's my Dad's garage. I was the only one of my sisters who was interested, so I learned all my life in there.'

'Amazing.'

'You don't know much about cars, do you?'

'I don't need to. I've got a good mechanic.'

'I'll teach you if you like.'

Boris smiled. He took a pull. The idea of him learning about cars tickled him a bit. 'You might find me a slow student.'

'I doubt it. Once you understand the basics, you just build on that. Everything's connected.'

'I'm in.'

She smiled. Took a sip. The music was just right in the bar, seventies funk was just the soundtrack Melbourne winter needed. Plus it was just warm enough when the doors weren't opening. Boris felt warmer than he had in days, at least until some other twerp walked in.

'Let's get another round and change spots.' Jolene was thinking the same thing.

'I'll hunter-gather the drinks. Can you find us better shelter?'

'I'll find us the warmest cave this bar provides.'

Catherine stared at the blue velvet and wondered how she hadn't done this shape earlier. On a long face, this would sing. On the right face, it would glow. These moments made up for all the misfires. Tom Waits said about art that sometimes you got the bird and sometimes you just got a mouthful of feathers. Today, she got the bird. She raised her fingers in clicks and felt the world spin slowly, just for her. In fact, she glanced outside to see the shadows lengthening. There would be food and nourishment of other kinds in just a few minutes at the Glasgow Palace – oh happy day.

Her phone chirped at her. Daring the damn thing not to be Virginia, she looked at the screen – it was Neal.

'Good timing, my friend. I have just finished work.'

'As have I, my dear. Would you like to know a story?'

'I would indeed.' Catherine put her feet against the blow heater under her desk and slipped off her shoes.

'Well. I know it wouldn't shock you to know that some successful people aren't really that successful.'

'And Mr Barwick?'

'He has that air of tragedy to him. He builds shops, he has lavish launches and seems to be at the top of Gippsland society. And yet. Three times in the past decade he has had to rebuild the company. Each time with another of his children listed as a business director. He makes money, but spends it faster, again and again.' Neal sniffed. 'Also, I suspect he was born quite rich.'

'Ah, the great Australian self-made man proves elusive again?'

'They're never quite as rife as we're led to believe. Though I think this is a global phenomenon. Don't beat up your own race.'

'Oh please, we're so easy to beat up. And remember, I'm rich, so I either beat myself up and stay in Brunswick, or pretend I'm superior and go south. And I like Brunswick.'

Neal's laughter was one of her favourite sounds. Like ice in a glass or a teacup on a saucer, it gave a sense of peace. 'So, I suspect that each time one of his businesses has a stumble he has to draw on some old money. I wonder if that's why his children get involved.'

'I don't quite follow, why would his children have money?'

'Inherited from his Grandfather, Franklin A. Barwick. Franklin actually was rich, coming out from Britain. Money in munitions, I believe.'

'You have done your homework.'

'That one was a quick Google search, you can read about him online. He had a contract with the Americans in between the world wars. Had a good head for business which didn't get passed all the way down the line.'

Catherine idly caressed the blue velvet. 'Okay, so Barwick is, as expected, a dill.'

'Yes. His father was more sensible, and you said it was he who gave Silver the money. Sadly, the father lent a lot of his money to Anthony, in his twenties, who has not done as well as it looks at first glance. It appears that Anthony's Dad's will was written so he could not get to all the inheritance before the grandchildren had their share. Mia was the last grandchild, born twenty three years ago.

'Should I take Barwick's money?'

'Do you need it? You're rich, right?'

'I'm a firm believer in Keynesian economics. I will take his money, and divide it between you, Boris and the Glasgow Palace.'

"I'll send through my invoice.'

'Do, you're amazing. Now I shall retire to my second office.'

'My regards to Boris.'

'Oh, he won't be there. He has that date.'

'That's right. The one he showered for. I forget the wiles of the young.'

Catherine hung up. She looked out the window at the coming dark. Thought about the Palace. There would be people to talk to and a distraction against the cold and the case.

Then she heard it again. The crack of Silver's neck, which reminded her why she kept going, though it was clearly time for drinks. Sometimes she had a job that even she couldn't ignore.

She walked around the block. Even though it was cold, she found these calls easier to make perambulating. This kind of work always got her steps up.

The number rang four times. Catherine was about to hang up when Jean answered.

'Hello?'

'Jean Foley. My name is Catherine Kint.'

'Ah, our saviour.' Jean's voice was even. This was not an expected response. Catherine stopped walking.

'I doubt it. I'm more a bad influence than anyone's saviour.'

Jean laughed a fruity laugh. 'I like you better already, then.'

'Jean I'd like to talk to you about the troupe. Do you have some time?'

'Do you know the training house?'

'Virginia's circus school in Pascoe Vale?'

'Yep. I'm here now. I'm training but I can talk.'

'I'll see you in fifteen minutes.'

Boris and Jolene had covered off some family history, career projection – or in Boris's case a cross check of his various misfires – Australian politics and the future of space travel. Jolene seemed delighted that he was interested in the engineering of space travel and Boris was thrilled that she didn't mind that he had most of his ideas through watching Star Trek. Dinner had also been delicious.

This was a night that Boris could see going longer. But he kept thinking about the bald man, and his friends. And he was keen to be getting towards the safety of home.

'One more, and then I'll have to make tracks.'

She smiled easily. 'Sure. Early start?'

'Probably. I do a bit of work with a friend on the side.'

'Oh right. What sort of work?'

'It sounds very exciting: it's investigation. But it's mostly me watching for people who don't show up.'

'Even that sounds exciting compared to changing a fuselage.'

'Yeah, but you can do that in space and it's amazing.'

'You can look out for things in space too.'

'I'll get the drinks.'

Boris tried to remember the last time a date was this easy. He couldn't. Then unbidden came the thought of Ciara kissing him last night. Between the date going well, winning a fight and a pretty woman kissing him last night, he had to strongly consider the possibility that he had stumbled into someone else's life. He scanned the bar. No thugs. The windows revealed Sydney Road, cold, dark, but no one and nothing particularly menacing. A tram rocked past. Not many people on it. It seemed everyone had the memo that it was cold and had moved into hibernation. Boris wondered if he had outlasted the pursuers. It seemed unlikely.

'All the more pints for me then,' he mumbled, taking the drinks back to their table.

Catherine had discussed several odd things in difficult situations over the years. She had spoken to friends in prison, lovers in hospital, any number of worried or desperate people, who either needed her help or had information she needed. As she walked into the cold, dimly lit training space – the door was open – she saw something new, which enhanced her Sunday no end.

This was the first time someone was hanging upside down. The hall was empty aside from Jean; who was hanging head-down from the trapeze on the northernmost corner. She was reading a book.

'Hello.'

'Hi.' Jean looked up (or down) from the weighty tome of *Medea* by Kerry Greenwood. Her blonde hair was loose, and Catherine was taken by the face that looked ready to smile at a moment's notice, dominated by the bluest eyes Catherine had seen in years. She was familiar, but Catherine couldn't pick why.

'So, why are you doing that?'

Jean looked at the book. 'Well, I like to read when I'm on a break. Don't you?'

Catherine raised an eyebrow. 'Have we met?'

'Nope. I don't know you.'

'Always read upside down?'

Jean dropped the book onto the crashmat, a few metres below her. 'No, I'm just hanging upside down as much as I can to build up resistance and leg muscle. So even on breaks, I'm a bat.' She swung upright, with a swiftness that made Catherine dizzy to see. Jean was unperturbed.

'You move very fast on that thing'

'I've worked very hard to be able to move fast on this thing. Thanks for noticing.' She flipped again. She made it look as difficult as blinking. 'What do you want to know?'

Catherine shifted on her feet. 'You know I'm looking into Silver's death. I thought we could talk a bit about you.'

'You don't want to talk about me. My break goes for another five minutes. Tell me what you really want.'

Catherine suppressed a smile. Strike one for softball. 'I wanted to ask about the politics of the group. I understand Ciara and Harley have some history, and your name keeps coming up as the most caring and least likely to be dragged into bullshit. What can you tell me?'

Jean gave a slow blink. 'That's more to the point – but why should I tell you, and how much?'

'I'm working for Virginia.'

'I know, she told me you would keep us safe. I already felt safe.'

'Yes. I don't think you need me to feel safe. But if you talk to me I'll have a better understanding of the group. And I may be able to find out what happened to Silver.'

Jean was upside down again. Catherine was aware she was being appraised. She didn't fight it. Sometimes it has to happen. After a few more seconds, Jean started talking.

'Have you ever been in a team?'

Catherine answered quickly. Eager to pass the test. 'Not for long, but yes.'

'Have you ever acted?'

'Yes, I did a bit at uni.'

'Circus is like both of those things and more. It's where the weird kids get to become superheros and make people gasp. But it's like being in an extreme sports team and a tight troupe of actors, where if you falter you can literally be letting someone down. A long way down.'

'So, intense.'

Her eyebrows flickered. 'Yep. There are egos, there are factions, but it's all about one thing.'

'Pushing yourself?'

'No.' Suddenly Jean was sitting on the trapeze rather than hanging from it, arms outstretched, holding the rope at shoulder length. 'That's sport,' she moved again, 'or, I don't know, transcendental meditation.' It's hard to shrug hanging upside down from a trapeze, but somehow Jean managed it. 'It's all about the show. The show is everything. So yes, Harley is a manipulative bitch; yes, Ciara is unpredictable; yes, Silver sometimes came to practice high; but it doesn't matter. Because at the end, it's going to be a show, and that's everything.' She had started a routine, swinging herself into various positions and manipulating her body. Catherine felt like she was being told a fairy story by some kind of human spider. The woman's arms must be like rope.

'So what are you telling me?'

Up she flicked, suddenly still and eyes level with Catherine. 'That I don't think what happened to Silver was murder.'

'Because it ruined the show.'

'Exactly.' She resumed her acrobatics. 'No one would mix her medicines up on purpose. The troupe had some issues, they all do. Frankly, I got used to people being mean in primary school. I used to sit and read by myself instead of giving in to the bullies. I still don't give in to them.'

'Yes, that's what Ciara said about you.'

'Harley doesn't bother me because she has no power over me, even though she was in *Cirque De Soleil.* Ciara and the others are all so scared of her. That's the information you'll get from the others. Various forms of justification for being bullied by a bully.'

'Why don't you stop her?'

'I stopped her bullying me. I try to help the others, but they have to come to it on their own. Plus, I work pretty hard to be able to do this.' She was doing a handstand on the trapeze, she wasn't even trembling.

'I understand. So you can't see any way someone would sabotage Silver.'

Jean was hanging from it by her hands now speaking as if she were at brunch while defying gravity. 'A circus person – and we're all circus people – just wouldn't.'

'How about getting in a bar fight after the show?'

'Yeah, that's a totally different thing. We're circus people, we're not saints.'

'So Harley made the big time. I didn't know that.'

'Yeah, but she lost it pretty quick. She improvised in a show that was supposed to be about balance. Upstaged her partner for the bigger prestige. She thought that move would make her a star, but it just showed she couldn't take direction.'

'Hence the reason she directed this show.'

Jean smiled. 'Virginia said you were quick.'

'Thanks Jean. That's all I needed.'

'Catherine, if you find someone betrayed the show, tell me first. Then you'll have an easy murder to deal with next week.' For a second, her face flashed angrily.

Catherine suddenly placed where she'd seen Jean before. 'Harmison.'

Jean went completely still. 'What?'

'I saw you in Sunshine. You were going to see Harmison, the physio, two days ago. You looked like you were about to commit murder then.'

'Oh shit.' The woman's face, already flushed with effort of training, went ruddier. She was an athlete, no question, but not a poker player.

'I didn't say you did anything wrong, Jean. But your face is screaming regret right now.'

Jean swung down. 'Ah. Maybe we should talk further.'

Soon after, Jean found some tea bags and soon they sat on the side of the training area, drinking tea out of glasses, which Catherine held on to with both hands for the warmth. The fluorescent light was on.

Jean was a sprawling type of person off the trapeze, and she sat with her legs far out in front of her. Staring into the space.

'I didn't sleep the night she died. Not just because, you know, it was horrible. I knew something was wrong. I spent some of the next day flicking through my phone messages from her. A few months ago, she said I should see Harmison. There was something in the way she mentioned him hooking her up with herbs that made me wonder if he was her drug contact too.'

'So you knew?'

Jean nodded slowing, sipping tea. 'Yeah, we all knew. We'd all had either our proud moment telling her to stop, or the coward one where we pretended we didn't know. I went proud.'

'How did that go?'

'First she denied it, saying that she hated big pharma so much she never even used Panadol. Then she told me she knew what she was doing. I made a few extra points. Then she told me to go fuck myself.'

'Ah.'

'Sometimes you know you won't change someone's mind, you just say it because that's what is right for you.'

The light was fading fast outside. 'So what happened with Harmison?'

'He denied it.'

'You believed him?'

'Well, I was threatening him with a pen knife and he didn't report me. So even if I don't believe him I think he's not a complete prick.'

'A pen knife?'

'I hadn't slept for three nights by then, I wasn't making good choices.'

'A pen knife?'

She shrugged broadly. 'It was the sharpest thing on his desk. I was aiming it at his testicles. I don't think he was lying. I gave him a lot of motivation to tell the truth. I half expected the police to come see me after that.'

'They didn't. What does that tell you?'

'You're the detective, you tell me.'

'I'm a milliner. But I think he's either so scared of you he didn't go to the police, or he had something to hide.'

Jean thought about that. 'Yeah, that makes sense. You'd think he would have gone to the cops if he was clean.'

'Yep.'

She put her glass down. 'I mean, I'm pretty sure I drew blood.'

Boris walked Jolene home, feeling safer for having company, even in the darkness. The streets were almost deserted. Only the light from the house windows they passed showed any sign of habitation. At some point, she took his hand. It felt strong and warm. Boris felt disquiet in his stomach and he hoped that Ciara was in her part of town and wasn't watching. It didn't stop him laughing or talking, but he felt suddenly hollow. He tried to shake it off, be in the moment, at the very least go through the motions.

Even the kiss goodnight didn't surprise or delight him, despite an appreciation for the technique. Of course, he knew all about technique now he was a player.

He knew she watched him walk away. It was easy and lovely. Boris chewed the inside of his cheek and felt like he had broken something even before he had found it.

He walked back through Gilpin Park, wondering idly if that wasn't the stupidest thing he could possibly do. It was wooded and there was just enough mist coming in to make it a perfect spot to corner him. He forced his hands out of his coat pocket and kept moving. He saw a figure ahead. A woman, walking in front of him, but going the same direction. She had a willowy figure. Boris immediately thought of Harley. But she was through the park and out of sight before he could catch up with her.

He thought of calling a cab. He could be home in minutes, behind the locks and in earshot of two housemates. Who, while they wouldn't protect him, knew how to dial 000 if it came to it. His legs kept walking even as he thought of it. Took out his phone and pressed. Nothing. He pressed again and remembered how low the battery had been. Flat. He swore, louder than he needed to.

He decided against crossing Clifton Park, even though it was more open and he would see anyone coming near him. It was still away from houses, roads and street lights. Also, just because a space was open didn't mean you couldn't be caught, especially after a long session at the Green. Boris rubbed his beard with fingers that seemed cold enough to snap off. He blew on them and kept walking up Albert Street.

After a block of no action at all, he found a sight that gave him pause. Outside one of the few houses was a slackline. Boris could see three hula hoops leaned against the weatherboards of the house. The light in the doorway seemed too bright to be believed. His guts did a small flip. Baldy had been sure about seeing him again. Boris turned sharply and surveyed the street. Nothing. No people walking dogs, no pursuers. Just a few more houses dotted in an industrial area. Well lit, but quiet.

He moved quickly for the next thirty seconds. Tried to focus on his breathing, the views, the sounds. Trying to be aware of everything but not overwhelmed by it.

So he saw the unicycle rider very clearly. A man. Boris didn't recognise him and as the man passed he didn't make eye contact, riding in the opposite direction. Hi-vis vest over the top of a leather jacket. It was enough, they were taunting him. Boris turned and watched him go around the corner. He hated unicyclists at the best of times, single wheel ego movers, but this was too much.

Boris started running. If he could make the train line he could hide out until a train came. He needed lights and people. He needed crowds and the police that came with them. He needed the herd.

He moved stiffly and he tried to recall just how many beers he had had with Jolene. He tried to find a rhythm. One two three four. Like Catherine had told him to. Like in football. Boris hadn't played football since primary school. Why was he thinking of this? He looked around, saw nothing. Possibly because he was only looking for a second. He got to the corner. No cars either way. Four more blocks to the train line. His breathing was getting ragged. He stole a glance behind. Saw the unicyclist. This time moving towards him, a hundred metres away. No other figures on the street. He looked at the houses he passed. Some of them were lit, others not. He could knock, ask for shelter. Charge his phone enough to get a cab. The thought of the slackline house came clear to his mind. They could be anywhere. They could be nowhere. His mind could be turning goofball circus people into gangsters in his head. The unicyclist wasn't catching up but was visible on the next block. Across the road, Boris caught sight of the same woman from the park. Couldn't make out her face.

His lungs were starting to burn. His throat felt two sizes too big and yet not able to get any air. Sweat was pouring off him, rolling down his face, stinging his eyes. Unbidden, he slowed to a stagger, bile in his mouth. He blinked against it. Beer is not a sports drink. He held on to a brown brick wall and concentrated on getting his breath back. Pushed himself upright and looked around. Unicycle boy had moved past. No sign of the woman. The train line was three hundred metres away.

Boris walked. One foot in front of the other. Three young men walked past on the other side of the street in Collingwood football regalia. They were singing, but it sounded more like Foo Fighters than football songs. He kept walking. Fifteen metres ahead was an alcove, a factory doorway. He widened the space on the path between him and it, increasing the angle of sight in case an attacker was there waiting. There wasn't. Just a dark space. Boris looked around. No one in sight but the three Collingwood kids. He slid into the alcove and took long breaths, becoming less ragged. He heard a train and wondered if he could make it. Saw it in the distance coming from town and knew that even sober and on his best day he couldn't catch it. The wind had whipped up and was pushing cold air against his face, which was wet with sweat.

He looked out on the street. There. On the corner he had stopped at a minute before. Baldy. Looking as menacing as ever, with his leather and his shiny head. He wasn't looking at him. Boris did the odds. If Baldy, Harley and the unicycle dude were all in it together, Boris didn't like his chances in a fight. He took a last big breath, thought of Jolene, and Ciara, hating himself, and ran.

12

We lost something important when we evolved to be so busy we can't hibernate anymore.
~Boris Shakhovskoy

The Glasgow Palace was busy, but not heaving. Catherine had digested Jean's story, a veggie burger and three gin and tonics when the phone rang. This time it was Virginia, but by that stage she was in love with the world enough to be generous.

'Hola, Virginia.'

'Hola indeed, my love.' She obviously felt no ill will from being shunted off earlier. 'I have news.'

Catherine shifted on her stool. 'I do enjoy news. Tell me what you know.'

Virginia's voice sounded small. Catherine pressed the phone to her ear and stuck her thumb in her other ear to drown out the pub sounds. She looked outside but it looked cruelly cold. Virginia's voice was bubbly. 'The police called. They have wrapped up their investigation. It's not murder.'

'Oh.' Catherine was suddenly unsure how to take that. Jean would be unsurprised. Surely that was good for Virginia, her client, even if Catherine herself had doubts.

On the other end, Virginia sniffed. 'Death by misadventure, they call it. They say that Silver's herbs had mixed with some sleep medication they found in her apartment, plus the effects of using opiates for some months. That would have caused the drowsiness that made her misjudge and…' She trailed off. 'Well, for her to fall the way she did.'

Catherine suddenly felt very, very sober. 'Oh, how awful.'

'I know. I don't know what to feel. I, I of course didn't think it would be anything else, but, well. It's still on me, isn't it? I should have noticed, or known, or something.'

'Do the others know? The troupe?'

'Yes. I sent out a group message before I called you.'

Group message. Catherine took her thumb from her ear and gripped the bridge of her nose. 'Did you speak with Ciara?'

'Not yet.' She paused. 'I will call tomorrow.'

Catherine hummed. 'She may need you earlier than that.'

Virginia's voice hardened. 'Right now I just want to take a pill and sleep for a week. I promise I will call her. I just, I can't now.'

Catherine watched the bubbles move up her drink. 'So I guess that's the case closed for me?'

'Well, yes, that's why I called. We know what happened now.'

'If you're satisfied with it I won't investigate further for you.' Which said nothing of Barwick, or Catherine's own curiosity.

There was a long exhalation at the other end of the phone. 'Catherine, you've been so kind. Please add a hefty bonus on for yourself when you invoice me.'

'That's not necessary, V.'

'I've been a mess and you've been patient.'

Catherine touched her belly, suddenly nauseous. The words "death by misadventure" had haunted her for a while now. She whispered a lover's name, inaudibly. 'It's really okay, no one's at their best when these events occur. Though Virginia, I did want to ask, do you know the name Jordan Harmison?'

There was a pause. 'I uh, he's a physio right?'

'That's right. He was treating Silver.'

The pause lingered. 'I have to go Catherine.' Her voice was final.

Catherine tried to stop her, but she was gone. Catherine watched the people in the bar and breathed deeply and futilely three times. She saw them in various states of happy, determined, loose. She watched the bubbles in her drink. She deliberately gave herself a few moments to notice things. The chatter of the people at tables. The swish of the post mix. The dull sound of Alyce's boots on the bar floor as she moved between customers. It was a mindfulness technique. A technique that did nothing to stop her thinking that something was wrong, and that this wasn't over.

Despite the burning lungs, his head still had its own notions. Knowing they were there made him run differently. It wasn't desperate, but he wasn't going to slow. In a minute he had got to the train line. Bounded up the pathway to the station platform. No trains coming either way. Five people on one platform, seven on the other. And some security. Some blessed people with authority and batons. Moving along the platforms and keeping the peace. Boris moved to platform two of Brunswick station. His gaze swung widely to take in everyone. Two families. One in Geelong cats jumpers on platform one. Three singles and a couple on platform two. No leather or menace to any of them. The Protective Services Officers were walking the far platform, wearing puffer vests in high-vis, guns at their hips. Boris took himself as far north as he could so he could see people coming in and out.

He was wet with sweat, which was quickly chilling even under his clothes. He couldn't see Baldy, Unicycle or Harley down any of the streets from where he stood. It was four blocks to the Palace, but he wanted to be home. The next train was only seven minutes away.

He smelled the rain before he felt it. A light dusting of cool water plastered his hair against his face. He stayed out of the cover, wanting the view more than the shelter. Knowing that if Harley and the goons came running he could cross the track and make a break for Sydney Road. The roads shimmered in the night, reflecting the street lights and the headlights around them. They always looked clean when they were wet. Boris was the only one not under cover at the station. He heard the hoot of the train going towards town and backed into the fence. If they were going to make a move, it would be now. It's what he would do in their place.

The city bound train flashed past on the opposite platform, then slowed, a blur of faces and lights. Boris kept one eye on the platform and another on the fence line. Harley could get over a fence like that easily. He didn't pretend to feel safe.

The train stopped. Rain fell across Boris' face. A man stepped onto the platform, thirty metres away from him. Blue umbrella, talking on a phone. He came closer. He seemed to be speaking in Hindi. Didn't seem to be concerned with the circus.

Two minutes until the Upfield train came in. The security guards patrolled the other platform. Boris knew they were watching him, and he didn't mind that at all. Yes, it was strange for him to be standing in the rain. Yes, they would keep an eye on him as he seemed odd, which was exactly what they were trained to focus on. It also meant that if someone attacked him, they would see that too, and hopefully not gloss over it.

He could see the lights of his train now, flickering through the precipitation. The people on the platform didn't move much; no sudden shifts that told him the circus had come to town.

The announcement came. Robotic and reassuring. 'The next train departing from platform two is, the six, forty two, to Upfield, stopping all stations to Upfield.' As it rolled in, Boris walked, approaching the doors quickly. He turned, wondering if they would appear and get on the same carriage, trapping him that way. The doors chimed a long whine as they opened. Boris looked into the carriage. Mostly people in football jumpers, quiet and looking at their phones. One leather jacket, red, on a young woman at the back. He stepped in, grateful. The doors whined again as they shut.

Boris watched the doors while the train started moving. Rain water trickled from his hair down his neck. It had probably been doing that for a while but he hadn't noticed. He held onto a pole and let out a long breath. He suddenly needed to pee and wanted just to be in his own bed for a while.

Seven minutes later he was off. He breathed and considered himself. A tired, slightly drunk man heaving out of the train and walking across the shared platform of Batman Station. The rain had stopped. Boris had just started to thaw in the train, but his fingers now told him he was back in the big chill.

He kept his hands out of his pockets They knew where he lived and he wouldn't be safe until he was home. Perhaps not even then. He walked out of the station and turned towards Ross Street. Across the road was a figure. Standing in a pink puffer jacket, hooded against the rain.

She looked jumpy, but agile, and Boris recognised the sense of stress moments before he saw her face.

He crossed the road to meet Ciara. She threw her arms around him and began sobbing.

Catherine had expected Barwick's phone call. She thought it would have come sooner. She knew what he would likely say. In fact, she had headed home from the Palace so she could take the call in a quiet environment. So, after she got home, dried her hair from the rain, and poured a gin, she sat and waited for the call to come. It gave her a chance to think – about Silver, about life and death. She thought about how humans construct clean words for messy circumstances. Words like "death by misadventure" and "friendly fire."

She must have been thinking hard, because the call jolted her.

'Hello, Mr Barwick.'

'Catherine, you've heard?'

'I have. I'm very sorry. How are you feeling?'

He sighed. 'How am I? I don't know. How could I feel anything but awful? That hasn't changed in days. I just thought we would find out what happened. I'm not convinced this is it.'

Catherine stood and leaned on the kitchen bench. 'I'm not either. Do you want me to keep looking into it?'

'At least until we know more. I also want to talk about her will.'

'Did she have one? She was twenty three.'

'I made all my kids write wills when they turned eighteen.'

When their trust fund money came in, Catherine thought. She looked at the photo of her Dad on the far wall. His bearded, bespectacled face smiling at the camera. Why did she call him so rarely when it was so obvious how lucky she was to have been his daughter?

'The police didn't mention it?'

'No, and worse, our family lawyer say Mia changed it while she was overseas. He doesn't have a copy of it, but knows she changed it because she called and asked for the old copy years ago. Can you believe he didn't tell me? What happened to loyalty?' He exhaled, seemingly as angered by this as the news from the police.

'I don't know.' Said Catherine diplomatically. 'Did the police uncover anything?'

'Not that they could explain to me directly.' He breathed hard into the phone. 'There just something wrong here, Catherine. I don't trust that circus owner, I don't trust the cops. Nothing is making any sense.'

'How's your wife?'

'Oh shit, Jenny. Don't even start.'

'Maybe you should be with your family, Mr Barwick. I'll keep looking.'

'I need to know nothing's going to come back and bite us, Catherine. I've already lost too much.'

'That makes sense.' said Catherine, wondering which part of it did.

'Thanks, and anything you find, just let me know.'

Catherine thought about telling him about Silver's burner phone, but that could wait. The whole thing could wait. The whole thing was making her want to go to bed and not wake up until someone else had done something. There was something so icky about all of these people that Catherine just wanted to be a milliner for a while. Dealing with these folks was bad for her chi.

She finished the gin. It didn't hit anything like the spot, but Catherine knew this mood well enough to know nothing was going to. Nothing would come close. Once upon a time that would mean destructive behaviour. But with the years passing, Catherine was learning that pleasure comes in many forms. Sometimes a walk is as good as a drink and sometimes exactly what you feel like is exactly what you don't need.

She drank water from the tap. Picked a book up from the shelf and ran a bath. She might think of the case, she might be able to forget about it, but she would be warm and clean and ready for tomorrow. Whatever that bloody meant.

'So it wasn't murder.'

'That's what they say.' Ciara was in Boris' bedroom, sitting in his only seat. Drinking his second last beer.

'Do you believe it?'

She kept looking at her feet, or at something in that general area. 'Who cares what I believe?'

'I do, that's why I'm asking.'

She smiled at him. There was something carnivorous about it that Boris really liked.

'I think there is more to this than an accident.'

'I agree.'

Her head tilted, just slightly. 'What makes you say that?'

'Well, for the first, it's what Catherine thinks, and she's the smartest person I know.' For a second Jolene flashed into his head. He ignored it. 'But the real kicker for me is that I've been followed by Harley and her goons for days now.'

Ciara jolted. 'You have?'

'Yeah, her bald henchman came a-knocking today as I left.' Boris showed her the slightly reddened knuckles on his right hand.

'Oh my god, what does that bitch want?'

'The phone, I think. Luckily I don't have it, so even if they take me it won't work.'

Ciara didn't move, and her face hardly flickered, but Boris could see she was processing a lot very quickly. After ten seconds she looked at him. 'Are you scared?'

'I was. Now I'm home.'

She smiled weakly. 'I want to be home too. I think it's time I went back to Sicily. Leave the fucking circus to Harley and her bitches.' She put down her beer on his desk and sat, shivering. Boris knelt next to her and put his arms around her. Aware of how much he'd run today, and how much a shower would help the situation.

'Sometimes I'm so afraid, Boris. Sometimes all I can see is endings.'

'Everything passes, Ciara. Just be here and everything will pass.'

After a few minutes, she stopped shivering and wept.

Soon after that, she stopped weeping and kissed him.

'Boris.'

He thought she had fallen asleep. Maybe him wondering about big Sundays was noisier than he thought. 'Yes?'

'I want to go home.'

He shifted. Her head was on his shoulder. 'Tonight?'

Her voice was quiet. Like she knew she was asking a lot, and wasn't sure if she wanted to be heard. 'Yes, now. Will you take me to the train station?'

Boris checked the clock. It was 9:50. 'Are you sure you won't stay here? It's cold.'

She was already out of bed and reaching for her clothes. 'I just want to be at my home.'

'Okay, but let me get you an Uber. Harley and her crew could be out there tonight.' He thought about the man on the unicycle.

She considered the idea in the darkness. He didn't push. He wanted to be alone, too. It had been quite the day. Two women in one day. He wasn't this person, and he hadn't really invited it. He tried to hold the thought. This would be easier to think about when he was alone.

Dressed again, they walked into the street. Ciara looked up at the clouds. Boris checked his phone for the approaching driver.

'They are pretty tonight.'

Boris looked up. The clouds were enormous, and moving fast against the cold night sky. 'Yes they are.'

She took his hand. 'I want you to know. You didn't do anything wrong. I just suddenly want to be alone.'

'I understand. I don't mind.'

'Thank you for paying for the car.'

'I'm sorry I can't drive you. I was drinking with a friend.' His stomach turned but he ignored it. 'It's really okay, Ciara.'

When the Uber came, they didn't kiss goodbye. Boris watched as the tail lights moved towards Sydney Road. The night was clearing, with a gibbous moon rising in the south-east.

Boris heard a scrape, and looked to the building site across the road. Saw the red glow of a cigarette. He turned quickly for home, but footsteps came up rapidly behind him and something heavy cracked into his back. Pain seared through him and he moaned, arching his shoulders. A fist struck his face.

He moved his hands up, vision blurring. His face was wet. He saw two pairs of legs and knew he had to swing a blow above them, but he couldn't quite shift his arms. He was aware of something coming at his head and then there was nothing.

13

Sometimes when you need a little magic, you get an abundance of gravity.
~Boris Shakhovskoy

Catherine wasn't surprised she couldn't sleep. This may have justified more gin, but tonight she just lay there. Listening to the wind and, for some reason, fixating on how you might play the theme from Super Mario Brothers on the harp. She had only the basics of harp and hadn't played Super Mario Brothers in years, but the awake part of her figured that at this point of the evening, anything goes in old brain town.

A tree was scraping her roof. Not her tree, her neighbour's. Catherine listened to the almost rhythmic scratch. She couldn't work out if it was a pleasant or unpleasant sound, she imagined an operatic mouse doing repetitive vocal warm ups, or perhaps a tennis player that had been shrunk mid-match. Wood on metal; influence and resistance.

She sat up. Blinked. Such thoughts were fun, but wouldn't lead to sleep quickly enough. She got out her note pad and turned a light on.

She wrote.

Silver died with recreational drugs mixed with sleeping medication in her system.

Silver presumably (she underlined this) used these sleeping tablets. (Catherine chewed her pen and wondered if she should get those things.)

I didn't see any pills in her bathroom

I didn't look in the bedroom properly

Jean said Silver hated Big Pharma – would she use sleeping pills then? Silver said this when Jean was asking her about drugs, so may be full of it.

Harmison may have given Silver drugs; Virginia knew his name.

Harmison said Silver was the only circus person he was treating.

Harmison didn't go to the police despite Jean cutting his testicles with a pen knife.

Who uses a pen knife? (She crossed this out: focus, Kint.)

Barwick turned up a week after Silver died.

Barwick is broke, or if he isn't probably will be again soon. And he knows this.

Barwick asked about her will.

Harley was friends with Silver, but not with Ciara.

Harley wanted to find something in Silver's house.

So did Ciara. (Catherine crossed that out. That had been her, Ciara had just followed her lead.)

Ciara was assaulted the day they searched Silver's house. (Catherine drew a line between this line and the one about Harley wanting to find something in Silver's house.)

No one saw the assault and Ciara wouldn't go to the police.

Virginia is clearly not in charge of the troupe. Perhaps Harley wants to split off?

Harley is watching Boris, doesn't know about me.

Harley acts like a person with a higher sense of self – i.e., high

Catherine tapped her pen slowly on the tip of her nose.

If Harley has the will and the means to stalk Boris, why wouldn't she put two and two together about me?

She was on the fourth tap when her phone started ringing. The clock said 1am. She didn't know the number. She shouldn't answer. It could only be bad news. It was only ever bad news at 1am.

'This is Catherine.'

'Hi. I have your Boris.'

'Who is this?'

'Bitch, don't even. Listen to this.'

The sound on the phone was of someone snoring. Catherine hated to admit that she recognised the sound immediately. Her left hand gripped her bedsheet as she stood.

'What do you want, Harley?'

'You know exactly what I want. Get to Batman Station in twenty minutes and wait for a call.'

The line went dead.

Eighteen minutes later, Catherine was in the frosty air. She was rugged up, but it still felt like the cold was trying to get inside her, through her very bones. A pale yellow light and the occasional passing car were the only augmentations to the view on a moonless night. The light played against the four rails that by day took trains either north or towards town, but by night just looked hard, and cold. If Catherine looked at them from a certain angle they gleamed.

Catherine was aware of the sound of her breathing, her rapid blinking, and how she was feeling absolutely nothing. It took her like this sometimes, almost like after she'd seen a body. This was better than fear: better for her, and Boris. There was nothing except linear, slow thought as her body stored its feeling for another time, a later, when feeling might be useful again. There was a tick of a clock from within the station itself. The wind was minimal.

A phone started ringing. Not her mobile, the payphone in the station itself. Catherine rolled her eyes. She thought they'd all been taken out and replaced with free wi-fi booths. Ridiculous. She paced up the ramp to the station platform, boots loud against the night's silence. The phone stopped as she got to it. Catherine breathed out. Turned around. It rang again. She answered it.

'Do you like this, little mouse?'

'This isn't a Hitchcock movie, you bimbo.'

Harley gave her high pitch chuckle. 'Oh, the little mousey one can roar.'

'Where's Boris?'

'I'm sending a van for you.'

'I'm not getting in any van.'

The laugh again. You could tell a lot about someone's nature by their laugh. Harley's was a weapon. 'Then I'll get your Boris.'

'You know I'm recording this.'

'So?'

'So I don't get Boris, but I have irrefutable evidence of who had him. You're not afraid of prison, Harley?'

'I'm not afraid, period.'

'Bully for you.'

Catherine heard conversation in the background, but couldn't make out the words. Then Harley was back. 'White van will come past in one minute. Follow us. Any cops and I–'

Catherine hung up. Clichés Incorporated could say that one to herself. The phone started ringing, then stopped. Catherine smiled as she walked down the ramp.

A police car went past. The cops inside didn't see her.

She sat on her Vespa and started the engine. It was one of the rare moments she would have preferred a more powerful vehicle, so that she could rev and possibly ram something.

Thirty seconds later, a van went past. Too hard to know if the driver was Harley, but Catherine wasn't waiting for a gilded invitation. She swung out behind it. Drove west along Gaffney Street. The number plate had faded to the point of being blacked out, so Catherine knew she was on the right track.

As they came towards the warehouses, the van sped up to take the corner into Williams Road, giving Catherine the briefest sensation that she was being watched.

Catherine accelerated, but a Vespa is not a pursuit vehicle. She roared into the night and followed the red tail lights. They turned left onto Charles Road, back up towards the industrial area near the train line.

Catherine caught up, swearing under her breath for six full seconds, but she saw no sign of the van. She slowed, then veered quickly, swearing, as the van flew out of a driveway behind her and tried to run her down. The backdraft pulled past her and she tasted the bitterness in her mouth.

Somehow, she hadn't ended up in the gutter. A light turned on in one of the nearby houses. She pointed the bike after the van and accelerated.

Now she felt something. It was unadulterated, white hot, anger. She was going to kill someone. Boris would be an afterthought, and he would understand.

Boris' nose didn't feel right. That was the first thing. Didn't feel right at all. There was pressure in all the wrong spots, his sinuses were heavy, as if underwater, but he wasn't, he could breathe. He swallowed to try and fix it. The swallow didn't feel right either. Then he registered the pain. Something had hit him on the face and possibly broken something. He tried to touch his face but couldn't. His hands wouldn't move. His body did though. It swayed. Like he was adrift. In space.

He felt the cold next. It was freezing. He tried to move his hands again: nothing. He pulled, and his body jerked. He was suddenly wide awake.

His hands were tied behind his back. His whole body swayed and lurched in time with his attempts to move his hands.

He blinked. It was dark. Only one light, far off. Halfway down a staircase that came down from the roof, in the wrong direction. Escher etchings crossed his mind before the swaying and the upside down stairs made terrible sense.

The stairs weren't upside down: he was.

With an unmanly sound, he looked up at his feet, his body bouncing gently. Tied up with a silken material which was held to the tin roof by an iron hook. Boris tried not to think of Silver's last moments. His breathing was very fast and he swished, trying to find purchase as his mind rejected the situation and screamed through every nerve that he had: danger, danger, danger.

He strained at the bonds around his wrists. They felt like cable ties.

Boris again made a high pitched sound, sobbing twice in the near darkness. He started moaning a denial. His breath came faster. He heard it, tried to focus on it, knew the only part of him that could move was his mind. He clung to anything that might make sense.

He thought of his parents, his brothers. Of Catherine. Ciara. Molly, his ex, came to his mind with a pang of annoyance. Telling him Catherine would one day get him killed. 'No,' he said quietly, shaking his head and closing his eyes, tears working past his eyebrows into his hair. Five deep breaths. He thought of Jolene laughing. Imagined her hand holding his, just a few hours ago.

He steeled himself to breathe slowly. Kept thinking of Jolene's hands. He smiled. He laughed. Any time the panic started back he took himself back to her. For a while, he could even ignore the cold. His face ached. He checked his teeth.

He was intact, for now. His feet weren't slipping at all. He decided he would give it a few more minutes before he started screaming. He could hear no traffic. He could be in a warehouse out bush for all he knew. He couldn't escape, yet, but he could fight the panic.

He wondered if Ciara had tipped someone off. Catherine would think so. He wondered why he was thinking about Jolene when Ciara had been in his bed since then. Boris wondered when he had become such a try-hard man of danger.

A real man of danger would be able to get out of this. Boris breathed as deeply as he could and remembered that this wasn't a movie. The fact that he hadn't wet himself should be celebrated. And he would celebrate if he got through this. Probably by sobbing for a week under the bed.

He heard a motor outside. Car doors opening. Closing.

'Hello?' he yelled. Voice higher than usual.

A door creaked open. A light illuminated the cavernous room. It was a circus training centre, though not Virginia's. In walked Harley and the two goons. Ponytail and baldy. Harley cackled when she saw him.

'Shat yourself yet fatty?'

'Look at that pig on a rope,' said Baldy.

'Piggy's gonna splat soon, eh, Mitch?' Ponytail had obviously also been to primary school.

'Hi, Harley,' Boris said. 'Only three on one? You must be getting braver.'

'Think you're pretty tough don't you, fatty?'

'Oh that's right, I'm tied up. Makes sense now.' He was aware of the moisture on his face from the tears. But his voice was even.

Outside, Boris heard the unmistakable sound of Catherine's Vespa and immediately the panic started to come back.

'Mitch, Tony. Grab her as she comes in.'

'I'll get her.'

Baldy – Mitch – stood behind the opened door. Boris noted their names. Always good to be on first name basis with someone trying to kill you.

Boris suddenly felt better. While Catherine being in danger was always terrible, these people assumed she was stupid. He'd seen this play out before.

A second later, beyond the door, Catherine screamed in pain. Mitch perked up like a dog hearing a new noise. He took a cue from Harley and walked out. A wet sound followed a few seconds later, accompanied by the sound of groaning.

Catherine strode in a good ten metres towards Boris before Mitch staggered in, holding his face.

If Catherine was shocked to find Boris upside down, it didn't show. She didn't make eye contact. She just took it in and stared at Harley. Boris knew why and almost smiled to himself. Eye contact created feeling and Catherine was in full work mode.

'Get him down.'

'I will. I just wanted you to see. Bitch.' Harley crossed to a bench covered in juggling pins, hula hoops and other circus props. She grabbed a large knife and threw it to Tony with the ponytail, who turned ninety degrees as he caught it to take the pressure off his hand.

'Get ready to cut a piggy down, Tony.'

Boris grunted, against his will.

'Don't be so stupid, Harley,' said Catherine. 'I'll call 000 and you'll all do time. Even if you hurt me, too. There's no gain for you.'

Harley grinned. 'Heaps of gain. I live in the moment. I like watching you squirm.'

'You want the phone.' Catherine reached into her bag. 'I have it.' She brought out her sealed Keep Cup. Black, with the letters CLK on the side. Boris recognised it; he'd bought it for her.

'You bring Boris down, slowly, or I give your phone a bath. You don't save things on the cloud, I hear, otherwise, you wouldn't need it so much.' She prised the lid off the cup, which she had filled with boiling water before leaving home. The rising steam was immediately visible in the chilly air. 'This is a $5000 bag, Harley. I got it for $30 in an op shop in Ballarat. I love it. But I think I'd love watching your face while I drown that phone and whatever is on it.' The cup of water was poised over the yellow leather bag.

Mitch moved closer.

Catherine's voice cut the silence. 'I can hear you dopey. Don't move.'

Harley's voice was low. 'Hand it over or I drop him. Ready, Tony.'

Tony raised the knife over the tissu where it was secured. Even Boris, who was trying to keep his mind blank, could see that Tony was sweating, despite the almost sub zero temperatures.

The silence was punctuated only by the outside wind. Boris' heart was beating in his ears.

Catherine's voice was completely even. 'He'd fall on his head. He'd be fine.' She tilted her hand, and a few millilitres of water fell into the bag.

'No! Fuck!' Harley screamed. She made a winding motion at Tony. 'Get him down.'

Boris screamed. Catherine jumped forward, sloshing water into the bag. Tony hesitated.

Harley yelled even louder. 'Slowly! Slowly. Bring the prick down slow.'

Boris descended, his eye glued on Tony's hands as they fed him towards the floor.

Catherine backed towards the door, making sure she could see each of them. Mitch's eye was badly bruised from where she'd hit him with the piece of wood she'd found outside. Tony was sweating in the chill. Harley had a look of sheer delight that was among the more terrifying things she had ever seen. The thought came: she is on stage.

Finally, Boris was on the ground, arms still tied behind him. He sobbed. Just once.

'What a wimp.' Harley snarled.

'Watch yourself, Harley. He's stronger than you'll ever be. Cut him loose.'

'Hand it over.'

'I will, but not yet. I see your friend still has his hands on the silk.'

'Tony, cut him loose once she shows me the phone.'

Catherine held the Keep Cup in one hand and picked the grey phone out of the bag. 'Cut him loose and I'll toss it to the mattresses.'

'Toss it to me or I'll string him up again.'

'Really? This again?' Catherine held the phone over the steaming Keep Cup.

'Fuck it. Tone. Cut him loose.' Harley's eyes didn't leave the phone. 'And the cable ties.'

Tony untied Boris' feet. Then he cut the cable ties on his wrists. Boris pulled himself up gingerly. Too slowly, but Catherine could see that his hands were completely numb. Tony tried to help him up. Boris grunted a swear word and pushed him off. He took a step towards Catherine and momentum let him reach her.

Catherine threw the phone into the air. Harley and Tony ran to catch it. Mitch lumbered at Catherine, who hurled the hot water at him. He screamed and held his face.

Catherine pulled at Boris. 'Can you run?'

Boris made a sound like a bear. Catherine took this to mean 'Of course.' They ran to her Vespa, Catherine pulling Boris behind her. He held onto her and climbed behind her on the seat. This was more weight than the Vespa was designed for, but it would cope.

A shriek rang out in the cold air. 'What the fuck is this?' Harley stood in the doorway, holding up the phone.

Catherine started the engine, Boris raised a finger, and they drove off.

Catherine kept an eye out for the white van's headlights, but saw nothing. At Williams Street, a police cruiser with its lights on but without sirens, turned towards the warehouse. Catherine chuckled.

Minutes later, they pulled into Catherine's garage and she half carried Boris up the stairs. He collapsed on the couch before she had even put on the light.

'Boris.' She leaned down, looking at his white face. 'Boris. Boris, you're okay. Would you like a beer?'

He gave a weak smile. She went to the kitchen. She was half way before the crying started. She turned back, sat next to him, held the big man while he cried long exhales of terror. She held him until there was nothing left, then again as the fear returned.

'I'm so sorry, my friend. I'm so sorry.'

He rallied, of course. Took a beer, then another, looking ridiculous in Catherine's dressing gown. He swore. A lot. Cried a bit more. Catherine did as much as she could to keep him laughing, but knew this would hurt him.

'Boris, you'll have to take some time to get through this.'

'I'll be fine.'

'Yes, but only with time. That was a prolonged, terrifying situation where you were completely out of control. It was different to the zoo, or the beach, or the skylight or any of them. In all those ones you knew you could fight. This time you were completely alone and upside down.'

He drank with some urgency. Forced a smile. 'So what, do you just get another Boris to work with?'

'Well, I spoke to Neal about cloning you, but he's dead against it. He's so smug about making his own humans he won't help me anymore.' She touched his face. 'Just let it get to you. It should. Christ, it almost got to me, seeing you up there.'

He turned away. 'I noticed you didn't look at me.'

She held his hand, with all the feeling she had repressed earlier. 'I couldn't. I'd have gone to water. I almost ran away and called the police, I was so scared.' Her breath caught. Tears brimming.

There was a long moment, before one of them started giggling. Soon neither of them could speak for laughter. Too loud, they tried to stop. Which made them laugh more, into cushions or Boris' fist.

14

Some days, survival is a victory, and all victory should be toasted.
Never miss a chance for dancing.
~Catherine Kint

Catherine woke to her phone. Virginia. She answered before her conscious brain registered how much she didn't want to talk to anyone. By then the Rubicon of discussion had been crossed.

'This is Catherine.' She cleared her throat, too late.

'Oh dear, I woke you.'

'That's okay, what's up?'

'Oh. I just had the strangest conversation with Mr Barwick.'

Catherine had blinked herself into semi consciousness. 'Are there any normal conversations with Mr Barwick?' Out the window, the sky was clear, but menacing; a sky that knew your secrets. That was probably unfair, given his daughter had died this week, but empathy came with coffee and she'd had none.

'Do you know anything about Silver's mobile phone?'

Catherine was suddenly very awake. 'Ah, no. What did he say?'

'He was talking about there being important documents on her phone.'

'How would he know that? They haven't spoken for years.'

'Oh dear. That makes it even stranger. The poor man seemed so wound up.'

Catherine put a foot out of bed. Brought it back in. 'You're sounding better.'

'I was so relieved when the police report came back. Did you know, and this will sound terrible, I was beginning to think that something awful had happened in my troupe right under my very nose.'

Catherine knew this kind of denial. Usually, it came from men, but here it was. Perhaps it was a sign that feminism was winning, that women could be moronic too.

'Well, if he's hassling you, I guess I should get ready for a call too. He asked me to look into things and he seems to be someone who calls people when he's at a loss. Vee, there's one thing I keep asking myself. Did the report really say Silver had taken a sleeping pill by accident before the show?'

'Oh no, they found it in her lungs'

'Oh.'

'They think she was grinding powders and got mixed up'

'Do take care of yourself. I think he's a dreadful man.'

'I will, thanks.'

Catherine lay down and watched the grey light move in again through her curtains. Another day, another gift.

She blinked as a thought she didn't like came to her. She spent the next twelve minutes trying to dismiss it by logic.

Catherine lay a pillow over Boris's sleeping ear as she did her best to make coffee quietly. She rotated her shoulder which now had only the slightest twinge, as he jolted awake. She wondered if he'd dreamt of being upside down.

'Good morning,' she said.

'Hi.' He was sweating, despite the chill.

'You all right?'

'No. I dreamt I was upside down again.' He rubbed his eyes, wincing when he touched his bruises. 'It's going to be a while before I enjoy the circus again.'

'Between watching Silver die and then last night, you're off the circus case for a long while, dear one. Coffee?'

'Yep.' He sat up, rubbing his chest now. 'I don't want to sleep again.'

'Maybe you'll dream of Ciara this time?'

'What? Oh yeah. Far out, I had more go on yesterday than I've had some years of my life.'

'I'm amazed you didn't wake up with white hair.' Catherine had to speak over the bubble of the coffee press. 'I'm about to get a call from Barwick, I think. Guess what he's after?'

'Hula hoop lessons?'

'Silver's phone.'

'Jesus. Him and Harley both. That scream as we left made me think that the phone we had wasn't it.'

'I suspected. I think it was a decoy.'

'Do you suspect who planted said decoy?'

'I do, but you won't like it.' She handed Boris the coffee.

His face was pale, he stared into nothing, not his usual look at all. 'Let's not talk about it then. I can't fight with you today. I'm busy being terrified.'

'Take a load off, soldier. I was scared too.'

The ringing of her phone ended that. She answered. 'Hello, Mr Barwick.'

'Catherine. I've been made aware that I need to find Silver's phone. The police have told me they never found it.'

'How very thorough of them.'

'Did you find it?'

She kept her voice even. 'No. What is on it that you need to get to?'

'I can't go into that.'

'I can't help you if I don't know what I'm looking for.'

'I paid you, Catherine. I appreciate that you're looking for the phone. When you find it, I want it to come to me. I'll send the same amount again.'

'Mr Barwick. I really don't think–'

'Catherine. I haven't always been straight with you. There's more to this, but I can only talk about it in person. Could I come to see you?'

Catherine looked at Boris. He looked like he really needed a day off.

'Yes, but not here. Meet me at the Glasgow Palace at 4.'

And he was gone.

Catherine put the phone down. 'I can see why he goes broke so often.'

'He wants the phone?'

'Either that or he wants to be sure it's gone for good.'

'Haven't these people ever heard of backing up their files?'

'Perhaps it's something clandestine?'

'That they both want? Boris drank his coffee and blinked. All his guesses were morbid. 'What are you going to do?'

'For the first time in a while I feel like "we've"–' she made quotation marks with her fingers, '– "done" 'enough. I think you should watch some television and try to get out of your head. I'm going to think.'

'Can I watch it here? I–' he stumbled on the words.

She smiled. 'Yep. You can use the headphones. I'll do this one solo.'

Boris hadn't wanted a second coffee. He seemed very small inside his own head. Catherine had him tucked up with his doona (which she kept in her linen press when he wasn't here). Made him a plate of breakfast and left him to watch science fiction with the headphones. She sat near him, drawing shapes on a note pad while she thought.

Barwick was full of shit. That much was clear. Yes, he was grieving, but he was also something else, which Catherine decided would probably have everything to do with money when it came down to it. Chasing money in large quantities was, to Catherine's mind, a symptom of having a lack of imagination.

Harley was less full of shit and more full of malice. She had an air of a girl who could do anything because she'd never been caught. When Catherine had threatened her with the police, it was as if the thought hadn't occurred to her.

Virginia and Ciara both had secrets. That was plain. To Catherine, it was clear that one of them knew something the police didn't, but whether that something had killed Silver, or was just a secret about the dynamics of the group, Catherine wasn't sure. She had spoken to both women a good deal in the past couple of days. They had both told her as much as they were going to, on pain of death.

Catherine blinked at the squiggles in front of her. Amazingly, they looked like a tree. Catherine wondered how she could make such wonderful hats – so she was told – and yet have so little talent in any other visual arts. She looked up to see if Boris had fallen asleep – he had not, and was double screening, checking his phone and watching the movie.

She moved the pen and drew a tissu hanging from the tree. Decided to let it move in the wind. Several factors create movement.

Everybody wanted Silver's phone. Which wasn't the one Ciara had found in the flat. So what was that phone? A plant? Something to make Catherine and Boris impressed with Ciara? Something to throw them, or Harley, or Barwick, off the scent?

Boris nudged her. 'Ciara wants to see me. Can she come here? She said she's scared.'

Catherine smiled lopsidedly, 'Are you sure? We don't know that she didn't feed you to them.'

'I'm sure. I'm even feeling better.'

The moment he had to care for someone, he could be brave again, or at least try to be. The man was as predictable as he was good.

Rain started outside and she watched a plane go past towards Tullamarine. It seemed inevitable. She gave Boris the big thumbs up.

'Sure. I'll trust your gut for once.'

'Maybe I should have that second coffee.'

'If she's coming over, maybe you should have a second shower.'

'Hey.'

'I need a walk, but you need company. You love birds hang tight.'

Boris' face fell. 'Maybe I should text Jolene.'

'Let that wait, amigo. One date doesn't mean you're engaged.'

He closed his eyes. She could see he hated this. 'Yeah, but it's not–'

'Just have twenty four hours where nothing terrifying happens to you, and then you can go back to the nineteen hundreds. Give yourself a break.'

'Twenty four hours. Okay.'

Catherine made a small bet with herself. Dialled the number.

One ring, two rings.

By four rings she knew what was coming.

'This is Doctor Jordan Harmison. I'm afraid I've had to attend to some business away from my practice and will not return to work until mid-October. Please leave a message and I will get back to you then. My apologies for any inconvenience.'

Catherine hung up. Croissants were in her near future. Boris could use some comfort.

Boris got up to open the door. Practically bounded. Catherine was back to thinking and doodling. Ciara looked wired. Dark colours under her eyes.

'Hey.'

'Thank you.' She embraced him, looking at Catherine over his shoulder. 'And thank you to you too, Catherine.' She extricated herself from Boris and looked him over. 'Jesus, your eye?'

'Had some action last night.'

Catherine sniffed into her coffee. They both shot her a look, Ciara a knowing one and Boris fit to explode. He recovered. 'Harley and her goons showed up after you left.'

Ciara's face paled. Catherine liked that; it was hard to do unless you were a very good actor. Her worst thoughts were quickly dismissed. Most of them, anyway.

Ciara touched his face. Boris winced, but let her. 'What did they do?'

'Perhaps you'd like a coffee?' Boris suggested, one eye on Catherine.

'Ah, yes please.'

Catherine got to making coffee as Boris relayed the story. Catherine listened to his telling. He'd started breathing faster when he woke up, but no tears. Catherine took this as a good sign. Even if it was probably buoyed by machismo.

Catherine passed Ciara the coffee – one sugar, she remembered. 'You two hang here. I need to stretch my legs and my head. I want to see what this all means.'

She gave Boris a "don't stain the couch" look and left them.

Outside there was sunshine. For the first time in a week, Catherine felt the almost warmth that came from winter rays. Immediately, she started thinking about climate change, and then if her generation was the only one prone to constant existential pessimism or if this was a human trait. Would her ancestors have seen early sun as a kind of hubris that God would make them pay for afterwards? Or did they simply till the fields, gather the animals and care for the children?

It made sense to think they, too, felt dread. Almost daily, about something they could only perceive but not understand. Maybe it's why they burned witches.

Why did we always think of previous generations as less intelligent? Sure, education wasn't as prevalent, but that didn't mean they weren't equally flawed and interesting people who were great protagonists in their own stories. Maybe it was because so much of what we remembered was the stupid parts, like burning witches.

Catherine tried to remember the name of her great-great–great-great aunt – Agnes, she decided after a few false starts – who had also been a milliner. She wondered if Aunty Aggie would have been up for breaking into a woman's car to investigate a murder.

She found Ciara's purple car around the corner. While there weren't many people around, there was no way she could force the lock unnoticed. So she made a confident stride to the car, did a small pantomime of having left the keys in the ignition, and with two hat pins and a neatly fashioned hook, was inside in less than forty seconds.

Now came the awkward phase of rifling through a car without changing anything.

The car was in such a state she wasn't sure where to start.

'Hi Catherine.'

She looked up and saw a neighbour's child on a badly timed dog walk. 'Oh, hi Fin.'

'New car?'

'Borrowing it from a friend.'

He looked in a window. 'Your friend is messy.'

'You're right. I might clean it up for her.'

'Seeya!' he skipped along the road in a way that was far too unassuming for a ten year old.

Catherine looked back to the car, half an ear out for an alarm – nothing. The car was indeed cluttered. In fact, had it not been for the circumstances, Boris and Ciara were a match. Only his beloved Ford had been this messy. Clothes, coffee cups, crisp packets. Catherine dived into the back seat and tried to look and touch without making it seem ransacked. The smell was almost like Boris' car, but with added perfume; the culmination of both the reality and fantasy of what dancers and acrobats everywhere smell like.

Catherine's hands waded through socks, various forms of plastic that once held food, primarily felafel, from what she was smelling. Under the passenger seat she found a copy of a paperback detective novel. She moved to the glove box, which was inexplicably neat, containing only an owner's manual and a box of tissues. There were no used tissues among the detritus and she gave Ciara a nod of tacit approval. Messy, but not feral.

Next to the hand brake was a plastic pocket which had once held herbs. She sniffed it, thinking she would smell marijuana, but it was a different, earthier. She slithered, snake-like, into the back seat. Put her hand under the driver's seat.

'What are you doing in there?'

Catherine's mouth went dry.

She looked up, not at Ciara, but a member of the police force. Young, male, indigenous. Catherine smiled weakly.

'Hi.'

'Is this your car?'

'Yep.' She held up the fistful of papers in her hand. 'Had to find some receipts, it's tax time.' She got out of the back seat, falling awkwardly at his feet. He helped her up. Locked the front and back door and hoped like hell the cop wouldn't ask to see in her bag, where her burgling materials were slightly clinking against each other. 'I really need to get a better filing system.'

The cop looked in the back seat. Catherine saw his bike on the other side of the street. Obviously part of the cycling patrol on Sydney Road. He took his time looking. Catherine realised this was the part where she said something stupid, so she didn't speak. Eventually, he met her gaze again. 'Yeah, you'll struggle to maximise your returns that way.' He smiled. 'Have a good day.'

'You too, officer.'

As he rode away, Catherine thought again about climate change, not so much due to the sun, but the searing heat coming off her cheeks.

She walked around to Florence Street and didn't stop until she was in the hipster café on the train line. Not that she thought anyone was watching her, but sometimes you had to get away from a spot of great embarrassment. It's the swift movement and escape that the brain needs.

She ordered a coffee and sat down, almost sinking her forehead onto the table. She allowed herself a small 'Yikes' and then realised being sprung rifling through a filthy car was small beans compared to what had happened last night. She supposed it was all a build-up. The mind must have an equivalent to lactic acid overload.

She spread the papers she'd found in front of her. One was a prescription for Stillnox, which made Catherine's nostrils twitch. The other was a paper serviette – unused. One was a shopping list, presumably in Ciara's own handwriting. Mostly fruit and vegetables. This was a bust, but good to have checked, Catherine supposed. She could get to Ciara's house and back in two hours. That absence would be extremely suspicious to Ciara and Boris, but she had to be sure either way.

Catherine unfolded the last piece of paper. She blinked, her stomach turning. She took two long breaths. There was only one appropriate response.

Just as the long macchiato was delivered she let go a long and heartfelt swear word. The waiter didn't bat an eyelid.

Boris spent the rest of the afternoon holding Ciara's hand, watching television and trying not to feel anything. He knew he was in too deep, he knew he had been scared and he knew it would be a little while before he wasn't scared again. The touch of Ciara's hand was warm. She hadn't spoken much, but had cried when he told her what had happened. That was nice. It's always nice when you find out you're scared, but with good reason. It's a comfort to not be an outlier.

Every seven minutes, he thought of Jolene. He'd remember he had twenty four hours to not make any decisions. He knew this didn't sit right anyway.

Catherine had come home with lunch in paper bags. They had eaten Turkish pastries, rolls and falafel until Boris felt full again. He had slept, with Ciara and Catherine reading, doodling, and not making much eye contact. When he woke they had a long conversation about going to the police. He noticed that Catherine gave no opinion, letting him mull the opportunity over himself. It was so unlike her that Boris felt almost discombobulated by it. He took her hand in the end and said, 'I appreciate you letting me make this decision – but we're too far in. If we bring the cops in, we might not ever know what happened.' He looked at Ciara, who gazed out the window at the gathering clouds. She caught his eye and gave a small smile. He had said similar things to her the other night, after she'd been attacked. Boris wondered if it had been Mitch or Tony who did that.

Ciara wanted to come to the Palace to watch over Catherine's meeting with Barwick – she hated him. But Catherine dismissed it. 'You stay here with Boris. I'll let you know what happens.'

Boris felt tired again after that and snuggled into Ciara's shoulder as they watched more television. She smelled like toast and sweat and warmth.

Catherine worked in her studio for a while, only coming up to change before the meeting with Barwick.

'You seen Boris today?' Alyce raised her eyebrow, an involuntary twitch that happened any time she was duplicitous, as she passed Catherine a wine.

'Nope. I think he's sick. He was feeling pretty rough last night.'

'Oh right.' Alyce moved away. Catherine had heard her grunt when Boris had called in sick hours earlier. Still, the place was hardly jumping. She could handle it.

Catherine checked her watch; 16:05. She sipped her wine, then wandered out through the dining room towards the beer garden. She hadn't noticed Barwick was a smoker, but maybe he'd taken it up in grief. He sounded wound up enough this morning to give heroin a shot.

Only Stevie was outside, Catherine raised a glass. 'Anyone else out here?'

He gestured with both hands. 'Just me on my Pat Malone, Catherine. Join a filthy smoker?'

'Sure, but I have a work thing coming soon, so I may disappear.'

'Hat thing?'

'No, the other.'

He gave a slow nod. 'So is Handsome turning up?'

'Nope. He's recovering.'

Stevie looked at her face. He was a good man with silence. 'You're feeling bad about something, sister.'

When he said it, she felt it, right in her guts, where she'd ignored it all day. The crushing sense of responsibility. For a moment, she retreated into her body, making herself small against the cold, against the world.

Catherine began to speak. She didn't know where the words were coming from. 'It's just, it's never me falling over. Sometimes I think I should take better care of him.'

Stevie took a long pull on the smoke. 'He grew up a long time ago, honey.'

Catherine smiled. Any man who called her honey needed to be

special or gay. Stevie ticked both boxes. 'Most people grow up. He seems to get hurt a lot for me. There's bad shit in the world. I run to it and he shields me.'

'If it wasn't you, he'd find someone else. It's his gift to the world. Heaven help the world if he went to the other side.' Stevie started rolling another smoke. Catherine pulled her jacket closer and sat down with him. The sky rumbled gently to the east.

Boris had fallen asleep again. The sound of the text woke him. Ciara smiled at him. She wasn't even looking at the television anymore.

He read the phone. 'Barwick hasn't shown up.'

Ciara scowled. 'It's after five. He is probably drunk. He is a stupid man.'

'You know him?'

'Silver told me all about him. He is the worst kind of Aussie.'

'What's that look like?' Boris thought of Barwick trying to hit him three nights earlier. He could imagine, but wanted an Italian's view.

'He is all about his family and being a cowboy,' she snarled. 'But he does nothing for his family, they were only ever ornaments to him. Such men are empty. And they hurt and hurt everyone to try and feel something.'

'Just an Aussie thing?'

'Of course not, it's half the men in the world, but I live here now, so I see it mostly here.' She nudged him and they kissed. It was the first time she had smiled in a while.

Catherine stayed at the pub, in part waiting for Barwick and in part to stay away from Boris and Ciara. Boris needed some time with someone to cuddle, and Ciara was obviously working through her own issues. Catherine liked the pub enough to give up her house for a few hours.

After it had gone six, Catherine dialled a number, fully expecting to hear a voicemail and order a gin, in quick succession.

'Catherine.' Barwick's voice was thick.

'I've been waiting for you, Barwick.' She let the irritation show in her voice, and "Mr" could see itself out at two hours late.

'I've decided, Catherine, that I need to take the matter into my own hands. If that bitch wants to try and ruin me, I know what I need to do. I need to finish this. For Mia.'

'Who do you mean?'

'My daughter.'

'No, Mr Barwick, when you say "that bitch". Who do you mean?'

'Someone who has it coming.'

Catherine stood straight; pushing against the tension she felt and feeling a small click in her neck. 'Do you mean Harley, Mr Barwick? Because I would not recommend that.'

There was a silence. Drunk people had terrible timing when they had to cover.

'Sorry to waste your time, Catherine. You'll still get paid, but I'll do this last bit myself. I need to get it.'

Catherine was gripping the bar hard. 'Mr Barwick, if you're talking about confronting her, I think at the very least you should–'

He was gone. Catherine tried to break the bar. Failed. Took deep breaths and focused on slowly releasing her grip. She stared around the candlelit bar. Amazed at just how stupid people could be.

Catherine ordered the gin, a double. She needed to think.

So Barwick knew Harley well enough to refer to her as "that bitch". Which was a horrible, sexist word, even if Catherine agreed with the sentiment. He was indeed a stupid, drunk, impulsive man. He had tried to hurt Boris, and Harley had actually hurt Boris. The police had found that Mia's death wasn't a murder. Surely those two could sort it out. Perhaps now was time to let go and trust in Darwinism.

Alyce placed the drink in front of her. She smiled thanks.

There were a few things that could happen. Barwick could confront Harley and hurt her: that seemed unlikely.

Barwick could confront Harley and get hurt: much more likely. How much did Catherine care? Stupid people got hurt daily. The only difference here was that she had met him and knew about it. Did that mean she had to risk herself to stop it happening? She crunched ice, unsure where she sat on that.

A noise entered her head, she hadn't heard it for a few hours, but it was back. It was the sound of a neck snapping. The sound of a life ending.

She didn't believe the police's findings. She didn't care what Virginia or Barwick had paid her. She didn't even care whether she was right or wrong about Ciara.

But she wanted to find out what happened to Silver, because she'd watched her die, and Catherine owed it to her.

So she made her decision. Then looked around the bar. Nothing had changed. This was a warm safe place and her decision meant she would leave it for a cold, dangerous place.

Sometimes our values made decisions for us that our bodies hated.

With a muttered swear word, she finished her drink and left the bar.

15

Bravery is when the child in you, and the adult, both ignore common sense, and agree to do it together.
~Catherine Kint

Any glow from the drink had been extinguished by the air around her, Catherine was walking alone up Mantell Street towards Harley's warehouse. How Barwick knew where it was, she had no idea, but she couldn't think of where else to look.

This was the deal she'd made herself: if Barwick wasn't here, then she would have no idea where to find him and she could go home, eat pizza with Boris, take Barwick's money and forget the whole thing. At least until another lead came along.

It started raining. She didn't have to check the forecast to know she was going to get quite wet. One look at the clouds and she knew that winter was going to push all the buttons tonight. She was already feeling the icy chill. The radio had talked about the blasts coming in from Antarctica. She believed it. You could almost hear the penguin chatter.

She came in view of the warehouse. The white van was there, indicating that Harley and/or some of the goons were home.

There was also what looked suspiciously like a hire car. It had bumped into the white van.

No pizza for now, it seemed.

Her phone rang. Boris. Exactly who she both wanted and didn't want to speak to.

'Hey, did Barwick turn up?'

Catherine kept her voice light. 'No.'

'Wanna come back? I was thinking about pizza if you don't mind us hanging out.'

She pursed her lips. 'It's not so simple.'

'Oh?'

Catherine swallowed. She should have lied. 'I don't think I should tell you.'

Boris' voice deepened. 'What's happened? Where are you?'

'I'm just looking into something.'

'Don't, Catherine.'

'I'm sorry.'

'Catherine, if you don't tell me I'll be so mad. You can't bench me for getting hurt.' He was at the edge of yelling.

Catherine scrunched her face up and looked at her shoes. Rain was trickling down her back. 'Okay. I'm just.' She thought of Stevie's words – if Boris didn't do it for her, he would find someone else. Catherine thought of Ciara and the piece of paper she had stolen from Ciara's car. 'Barwick's confronting Harley. I don't know about what. I'm at her warehouse.'

'Oh. All right.' As expected, all the fire had gone out of his voice.

'It's too soon, Boris. I'm not benching you, it's just too much to ask, even you. I can do this alone.'

'That's not the point and possibly not even true. I'll come.' Catherine heard Ciara in the background. 'We'll come.'

More rain ran down her neck; suddenly it felt like a relief. 'I knew that if I told you, you would.'

'Yep, so I'll see you in fifteen. Try to keep dry.'

Catherine hung up. Didn't wait. There was too much to see. The rain would give great cover, so she sidled along the side of the warehouse to one of the filthy windows on the north side of the building. Thankfully the slant of the rain was coming in south so Catherine could see inside. Harley, standing, was looking down at something. Mitch and Tony were either side of her. Catherine had the feeling they were standing in front of a very drunk and very angry middle-aged man.

Boris took a deep breath, squeezing into Catherine's biggest coat, still not having gone home for his own clothes. He looked at Ciara, who a second ago had been full of bravado. Now suddenly she looked small.

'You don't have to come.'

'No. I have to. Especially if Barwick is there.' She stroked Minty, who purred under her fingers. Boris was uncomfortable, knowing that Catherine didn't trust her.

'You wanna see him?'

She moved forward. Kissed him lightly. 'He is a stupid man. I knew that he would try to end it. I thought it could be,' she waved an arm, 'all blown over.'

'What are you talking about?'

'I'll tell you later, Boris. Let's say I have been given a secret weapon.' She took up her coat. 'Let's go, we have to help Catherine. She's too stupid to survive this without you.'

Boris was too confused to feel scared. The door closed behind them with a muffled bump.

Catherine walked around the warehouse looking for shelter. About two metres from her was a space where the cladding had fallen off, creating an exposed part of the wall, with a thin layer of steel between the elements and the factory floor. Catherine wouldn't be able to see, but if she pressed an ear against the wall here she may hear something. Mostly the roar of the metal roof being pelted with rain.

Harley's voice was two parts playful, one part venom. 'I think you should think about giving a little more.'

'You've had enough. I could have you done, trying to hurt my family.'

'I never hurt Silver. I had nothing to do with it. I never knew anything about the herbs or the pills. I just knew she was going to give you money and I thought she could find a better cause.'

'But we had a deal.'

'Then I thought better of it.'

Barwick let out a mangled scream. 'I don't think you even have it.'

The rain was sliding down Catherine's neck, wetting her back and even down to her tights. She should have been shivering, but she wasn't. She was riveted.

'Oh, I've got all the things I need, Barwick.'

'Hey. Get your fucking hands off me. Hey. I'll call the police. I will call the fucking police.' Barwick was screaming, but the fear in his voice would just feed the power lust in Harley. Catherine decided she couldn't wait any longer. She moved to the door and opened it. It wasn't even locked. Harley was bolshie as hell, but a complete amateur.

'Let him go, Harley.'

Harley looked at Barwick to Catherine and back again. 'Do you just protect all the fat white men of Melbourne?'

'He's not from Melbourne.' Catherine pointed at Barwick. 'And Boris isn't fat,' she added.

Tony and Mitch still had hold of Barwick. Barwick tried to break their grip, but couldn't.

'So this is all about money, huh?' Catherine pushed wet hair out of her eyes. 'He wants his daughter's money; you want his daughter's money. You were both close to getting it and then the accident happened. So what was on the phone, Barwick? Blackmail material? You playing away from home? Something to upset the local shire?'

'What? No, no. It's not like that.'

'So it's something stored on a phone. Let's see, a code for a safe. No, who uses cash these days?' She paused, playing for time, but also with an idea. 'Is it Bitcoin? Is that it?' Harley sneered but Barwick's head fell. Bingo. 'Bitcoin. All of Silver's lovely money. Enough to buy back the farm. Are you working with Harley too, Barwick?'

'Catherine, it's…' He couldn't go on because there was nothing to say.

Catherine pointed at Harley. 'So she raised heaven and earth trying to get Silver's phone. Because you had a deal. And she got a phone, but it wasn't the right one, was it Harley?'

'You don't even have the fucking phone?' Barwick screamed, breaking the goons' grip and charging towards Catherine – and the door.

'I'll find it!' Harley yelled as Barwick tripped over, wincing as he came down hard on a knee. 'I only know one place it might be, and trust me, I'm going there next.'

'To me,' said Ciara, walking in, Boris behind her. 'To try and find this?' She brought a red cased smartphone out of her pocket. 'This phone? Her phone. The one with the accounts on it? You all talk of her, but she's just money to you. You know what? I loved her.'

Harley turned to Tony. 'Go close the gates. All of us will have a talk and I don't want anyone getting away.'

Barwick looked fit to kill. He pushed himself up onto his feet again. Staggered towards her.

'You. Finally. The fucking dago, I'll fucking–' He ran at Ciara, but Boris stepped in front of her and nimbly jabbed him in the chest. Ciara turned to the doors, but they were blocked by Mitch and Tony, so she pushed past Barwick towards the stairs and the upstairs office. Boris gave chase but was too slow.

Barwick was more sprightly and moved faster than Boris.

'Boris!' Catherine called.

'I have to help her.'

They ran together. 'Yes you do, but I have to tell you–'

'Later, Catherine.'

He looked back, and she could see that he had guessed what she wanted to say.

Ciara had entered the office and locked the door. Barwick was pushing and ramming it with all his might.

Boris came up the stairs to see Ciara had found a ladder and was climbing to the ceiling of the office. There must be a hatch in there, which led to the warehouse rooftop.

'Barwick,' Boris called, bearing down on him.

Someone's footsteps sounded hard on the stairs below him, he turned a second.

Barwick's punch came quicker and harder than he would have believed. Straight into his guts. Boris went down on the floor of the mezzanine. The pain was immense, but his reaction was more about the surprise and the fact that he couldn't breathe. All he could do was watch Barwick's boots as he hurled himself at the office door.

The door gave way with a mighty crack and then Barwick's bulky frame was moving up the ladder. Boris knew he had to get up.

Catherine was in front of him. Harley seemed happy below, but Mitch was climbing up as well.

Catherine ran to Boris, but he waved her on. 'Get up there. That creep is going to kill her.'

Before she was even halfway up the ladder, Catherine felt the rain on her face falling through the open hatch. There wasn't much light on the roof. It was about thirty square metres of corrugated iron, with the hatch coming on the southern side. Catherine could make out the fencing and the train tracks behind. Ciara was on the edge, twenty metres away, looking down, and Barwick moving towards her.

'Barwick. Leave her be.'

Barwick took no notice but continued to approach Ciara. 'Give me the phone.'

Ciara was defiant. 'Back off or I throw it onto the train tracks.'

He slipped, slightly, caught himself. Catherine realised Ciara's advantages. Sobriety and being an acrobat.

Barwick clearly had no such thoughts, as he bellowed, 'Give it to me. Don't mess with my family anymore, bitch.'

Ciara straightened, rain pouring around her. She placed Silver's real phone in her back pocket. 'Come get it. Silver fucking hated you.'

'Her name is *Mia*,' he bellowed. Barwick ran the last two metres.

Ciara disappeared over the side. Barwick, still running, did too, his battle cry morphing into a yell of realisation; then a wet thud above the rain. And a silence.

Catherine walked carefully to the edge, her mouth dry. She kneeled there to look down. In the dark it was hard to see what had become of Barwick, but no sound came from the ground.

Boris came up behind her just as she saw two hands clutching the guttering of the roof. With his help, she pulled Ciara up.

Finally safely on the rooftop again, Ciara grimaced. 'Thank you. I knew you would help me back.'

Catherine smiled. 'Five minutes of lactic acid right?'

Ciara smiled weakly. Boris held her, but took out his phone. 'I think it's time to call the cops.'

Ciara's face looked pale, even in the cold. 'No, you can't.'

'I don't see how we get past the goon squad without them. There's already a man dead.'

'You can't,' Ciara repeated, voice higher.

Boris spread his hands in entreaty. 'Why?'

Catherine was cold, and wet, and tired. 'Because Ciara knows how Silver died. She knows who put the sleeping pills in her drugs. She's had Silver's phone the whole time. And she knows who planted the decoy phone, and the pills packet at Silver's house. Don't you, Ciara?'

Catherine produced the piece of paper she'd found in Ciara's car. 'I found this receipt for a burner phone in your car, a Nokia. It's dated a week ago. You loaded all those messages on the night before we went to Silver's house. You've been stringing us along.'

Ciara stared at the receipt.

'Is that, true?' Boris asked – though his tone made it clear he already knew the answer.

Ciara turned, looked below and jumped.

Boris screamed a no. She disappeared into the wet darkness. As they got to the edge they saw her take the last shimmy down a water pipe and a second later she was over the fence..

'Jesus.' He turned to Catherine. 'I can't do that, let's get down.'

'I'm calling 000 first.'

'You do that. I've got to find her.'

Boris ran to the hatch as Mitch's head stuck out of the opening. Boris kicked him and watched him fall. Boris leapt through the gap, ignoring the ladder and landing on top of the bald bastard. Who crumbled. Boris considered giving the prick a knee to the balls but pushed past instead. Harley was coming up the stairs and tried to block him, but he was thirty kilograms heavier, and this time gravity was on his side. He pushed her aside and she fell, yelping.

Crossing the floor, he stole a quick look at the tissu hanging from the ceiling to the middle of the floor. Then he reached the door and ran out into the night.

Tony was at the gate with a bat in hand. Boris ran to the fence that Ciara had gone over. Tony came after him, swinging the bat.

Boris stopped and pointed at a lumpy shape in the darkness. 'Know what that is?'

Tony swung, Boris weaved away. It wasn't close, but Tony's swing moved him closer to the lump. That's when he recognised Barwick. He swore, long and quietly.

'Cops are on their way, cowboy. You gonna be here with a bat when they come?'

Tony threw the bat over the fence and ran hard for the gate.

Boris climbed the fence to the train tracks on the other side. There was no train coming either way on the single shared track.

He stood in the rain, thinking. If what Catherine said was true, then he didn't want to find Ciara. He wanted her to get away, back to Sicily, off to Jupiter, anywhere but where she would end up.

Then he thought of Silver's death; and of Ciara, scared in the dark, in a storm, all alone.

He chose a direction and trotted towards Batman Station, probably because it was closer to his house and humans gravitate to what's familiar. Thunder boomed above him and he almost jumped, but it was as if his nerves were done and nothing was going to move him. He just ran in the rain, trying to find a woman who had done something wrong. How wrong, he didn't know. But he knew he cared and didn't want her to die when two people already had.

Boris slowed. Even though he had slept part of the day, he was exhausted. Maybe this was when he let go. Maybe if he went back, he could say to Catherine and the police, 'I lost her.' Maybe that's what she wanted. Maybe that's what she needed. Maybe it was what *he* needed.

He was almost at the station when he heard her crying.

Catherine was careful coming down the ladder. Mitch was in a seat, bleeding. Harley was sitting on the stairs, breathing heavily and holding her side. Neither of them made a move to get her. There was defeat in the air for both of them.

'So you wanted his money, for what, your own school? That's what this place will be right?'

Harley scowled. 'He came to me six months ago. Wanted me to help get Silver to reinvest her trust fund into the family business. The guy was a fucking creep.' She cracked a knuckle. 'No wonder I had to work her so hard.' She smacked Mitch's bald head. 'We gotta go, these girl scouts have called the cops.'

Mitch groaned, but moved.

Catherine took that in. She couldn't imagine ever thinking like that, especially so easily. 'What about Ciara?'

Harley drew herself up to full height. 'You gonna try and stop me, little mouse?'

Catherine didn't draw herself up to full height. She didn't need to fight them, or intimidate them. Harley took Mitch's arm over her shoulders and moved. She was strong, no question.

'What about Ciara?' Catherine repeated.

'She's got her own Daddy issues, and took it out on Silver. I don't know how she did it. But I know she did.'

Catherine enjoyed watching Mitch's blood stain Harley's top as she slowly helped him down the stairs. 'But you didn't kill Silver?'

Harley grunted. 'Why the fuck would I do that? It ruined the show. My show, I directed it.'

'So what were you looking for at her house after the accident?'

'We've talked enough little mouse.'

Ciara was huddled under an ornamental pear tree whose branches stretched over the fence of a house. Boris sat with her. She was holding herself and looked exactly like someone who needed a friend. He held her.

'Did you kill Silver?'

'Boris.' She looked at him. "Boris. She was going to throw everything away. All the training, all her money. All she had done, so she could go back to her stupid fucking father.'

Boris heard the words, but couldn't believe she was saying them. 'So, you…?'

'I didn't know she would die. I just wanted to mess with her the worst way, through the performance. Circus people give everything for the show – it's all that's real. She was betraying me, for Harley and for him. So I wanted to take away the show. I mixed kratom into her ginseng for her tea. And, then, sleeping tablets into her speed.'

'What's kratom?'

'It's a drug from Thailand. It heightens you, but can also slow things down. She was using so much I thought the kratom wouldn't work. So I used the pills. I thought she would fall a metre. Then Harley changed the show at the last hour. She fell a long way. I knew she would snort out of her locker before the show. I tried to steal it back, but it was too late. So I took her phone so Harley wouldn't get the money.'

'So you mixed it.' Boris slumped. 'You poisoned her twice.'

'She smiled at me while we climbed the rigging to the silks. I thought maybe she would be all right.'

'You could have warned her.'

Her face showed him that she knew. She would relive that moment until she died.

The thunder rolled, further away from them now.

'How do you even know about kratom? I've never heard of it.'

'I take it when I'm tired. Virginia, she hooked us up for it with a physio.'

Boris thought about the far-away look Ciara got in her eye sometimes.

'So why bother with the other phone? The one we found in Silver's flat?'

She cried. 'For you.'

Boris blanched, rain falling across his face. 'For me?'

'The day after she died, I didn't know what to do. I was coming to tell Virginia what I did, but you were there and I knew that you would keep me safe. I–' She looked at him, intense, wracked with pain 'I felt you were the only thing that could save me. I just felt it.

She took a long breath. 'I thought if there was enough confusion, we might just get through. And I wanted you to protect me, from Harley. She would be looking for Silver's phone. I had bought a phone two weeks earlier and I decided I could make it a decoy. I made messages on it, so it would look real, like it had been used, I didn't know yet when I would need it. If I planted it for you to find, you would keep it safe. And me too. And when we broke in to her house, I left the packet of pills there so the police would think it was hers

Boris held on to her as she convulsed twice.

'I only brought the real phone tonight, when I realised I could ruin Barwick by breaking it in his face. He was so bad to her, Boris. But she was going back to him. Harley was making her.'

Boris held her tighter. Wondering why he could do this when she had lied to him, like that didn't matter. 'She's horrible, isn't she?'

Ciara scrunched her face. 'She's the second worst person I've met.'

She shuddered as the sirens approached.

16

So far life has been measured in scars, laughter, and regrets.
~Boris Shakhovskoy

Counting days. Boris was good at it now. Now there was only two weeks of calendar winter left. Twenty six had passed since that night on the railway. The night his life became both calmer, and yet more scrutinised, as he was a witness in a murder investigation. In the days following the warehouse incident, Boris had had his fill of police stations. The questions, the questions repeated, the bad coffee. Sometimes Harley or one of the goons passed him in the hall. No one smiled.

Through those questions, he learned things by how they were asked. Questions about the phone. About bitcoin and what he knew about it. Catherine had spent longer in interviews, as she had seen Barwick fall. She heard the questions too.

A little digging later, they found out bitcoin needed a person's phone or username to get the money. It was a poor product for dead people. They learned that Barwick had gone to Harley to bring Silver back to the family.

Boris thought of the night Barwick attacked him. Had Harley been watching?

The court date wouldn't be for months. So now, it was a holding pattern. A cold, monotonous holding pattern.

Boris had gone back to work. His face had healed. The nightmares were bad for a while, then he'd spoken to a psych, at Catherine's insistence. The nightmares weren't gone, but he was managing. The psych hadn't told him to see less of Catherine, and that was meaningful to him.

He'd learned a few things in those sessions. He'd talked, the psych had listened and told him what she understood about the story of his life, as he told it. About duty, and wanting it. About being defined by it. Of needing to be needed, and focusing his entire existence around it. There were things he'd spoken about that he hadn't told anyone, not even Catherine.

Now it was Wednesday. He was on a train, like most Wednesdays now. There were ten stops from his house to Southern Cross station. The remand centre was a one kilometre walk from there.

He came here each week. To fulfil a promise. A promise that legally he couldn't keep. While on the night of the arrest he had said he would visit, a quick word on criminal procedure from his lawyer Ben told him potential witnesses and alleged criminals don't sit and take tea together in any circumstances.

So each week, he took the train in, and sat outside. Just in case she could see him. He had assumed Catherine would tell him it was a bloody stupid idea, but she didn't. Sometimes he wrote in his diary – a new, therapy thing. Sometimes he just sat. He thought about what had happened. Why everything hurt. What he could have done differently.

His therapist, and Catherine, said he'd done nothing wrong. Maybe that wasn't the point, maybe it was just that something had gone so incredibly wrong. Blame seemed secondary.

He couldn't see a damn thing through the windows. The whole building gave him the yips.

So much suffering. Two lives wasted.

After the arrests, after the station, Boris told Jolene everything. They sat in a café, and she listened. She took his hand when he talked about being strung up, upside down, in the silks. She let go when he told her about Ciara coming the next day. She heard the whole story. She didn't interrupt. He tried hard to be truthful. She deserved at least that. Then she suggested a walk. It wasn't raining. Boris went to pay and found she already had.

They walked in silence for a while. Finally, they sat under the bare trees of Warr Park. Boris was completely spent. His brain told him to apologise. His mouth couldn't, because he didn't have it in him to do anything.

Jolene smiled. Then asked him one question.

'When you chose her over me, was it because you liked her more?' Once she had said it, she looked away. Her profile was the most beautiful thing he had ever seen.

'No, no.' He leaned forward, rubbing his swollen face with his right hand. 'I was just. She just.' He took a breath. 'She needed me.' His turn to look away, so he couldn't see her expression.

'Do you ever think about what *you* need?'

This deserved an honest answer.

'I, I think I just want to not hurt anyone.'

She shuddered like he'd hit her. A tear ran down her cheek. 'But you do, Boris. You do. You hurt people and you hurt yourself because you don't know what you want.' She stood. 'You've got to grow up, Boris. I can't do it for you.' She looked down at him on the bench. 'If you ever want to live well, you have to know what you want.'

He couldn't speak. He held a hand out to her, but did not, could not, get up.

She took two steps back. Her lips trembled. 'Call me if you work it out, and if what you want, really want, happens to look like me. I won't be waiting, but try your luck.'

Weeks later, when he thought of that, he cried. Quietly. A big man crying on the train on the way home. He told himself it was part of the PTSD, but he knew it was something else. She'd known his secret. She'd worked it out before he did.

He'd never been so found out, and so lost.

Catherine sat in the beer garden of the Palace, feeling the air around her because she could, and because she wanted to. Silver's death, and everything that came after, had been hard to shake off, because it felt even more like a waste than usual. There was no glory anywhere, just lives cut short and people hurt. The tragedy seemed as inescapable as the cold, she'd decided, until she read a word that freed her from trying: surrender.

She sat with that word, and that idea as something beyond cowardice for the first time. It soothed her, even if she didn't subscribe to it yet. She liked the idea of "not fighting" as an option. Surrender to the horror, the cold, the lies and the horrible fact that those who love you may one day die for you.

All you can do is be ready to do the same for them, to love them on the days you don't and for God's sake, don't be too serious.

Boris walked towards her, drinks in his hands. Smiling without teeth. Since the silks, Boris had liked being with Catherine alone, in a place with fewer people. He always had liked being with Catherine, but he hated being fearful of people. He hoped it wore off soon.

Boris put down the drinks.

'I'm still thinking about it each day. More than anything, it was a performance,' said Catherine.

Boris looked at the sky. 'Which part?'

'All of it. They gave everything for their performances, they had nothing outside of the stage. Barwick did the same, but the world was his stage, and he didn't have the moves.'

'Maybe that's why the circus people love it so much. Why need the world when you can rule a stage?'

Catherine looked at him. She saw him, all of him. 'I'm glad we don't need a stage.'

The clouds parted. And just for a moment, the sun shone.

HUGH McGINLAY

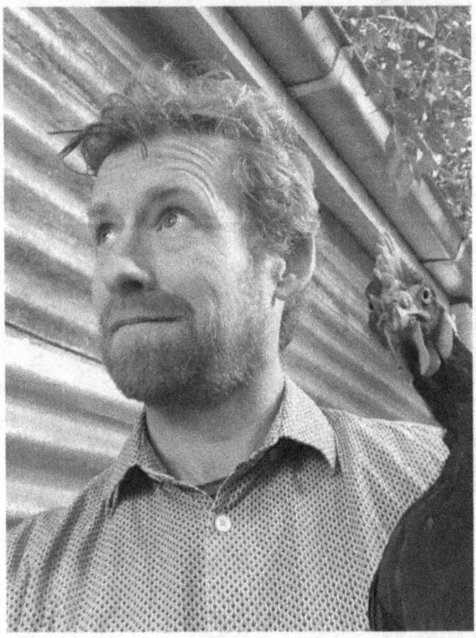

Hugh McGinlay is a writer, musician and optimist. These poor career choices means that he has also worked as a bus driver, a kitchenhand, singing teacher and a seller of dental consumables.

Now four books into the Catherine Kint series, he continues to be amazed at the levels his imaginary friends have been accepted into other peoples' heads and bookshelves.

As a musician he has released four albums and occasionally gets played on the radio. He lives in Melbourne with his wife, two children, a cat and several chickens.

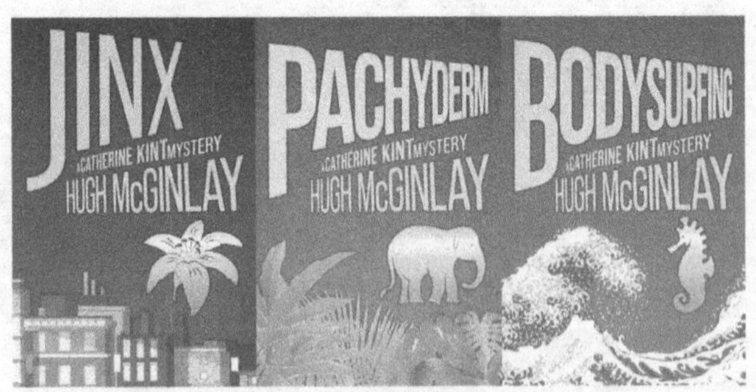

ACKNOWLEDGEMENTS

My heartfelt thanks first have to go to my friend and Publisher Lindy Cameron. In publishing, like war, it's good to be next to someone who's smart, tough and funny. Lindy is all those things in spades.

I was thrilled to work once again with Narrelle Harris, of the eagle eye and razor sharp mind, who gave this book the last cuts and touches before it could be unleashed upon an unsuspecting public.

My partner in crime (writing) Adam Palmer gave frank and fearless advice, pointed out what was wrong, and came armed with solutions to every draft and every discussion. Having his intellect, insight and natural grasp of storytelling on board has made this a much stronger book.

Geoff Dunstan is, according to many, a legend of Australian circus, having him as a friend and confidant on this project was an easy extension of him being a friend and confidant in all aspects of my life. A situation I'm very grateful to have.

Once again, I came to my brother-in-law Hans with a hole in the story, and his knowledge filled it up perfectly. Having someone in the family who's an expert in poisons and toxicology really reduces the legwork on a lot of my research.

All mistakes are entirely mine. I hoard them.

This story is dedicated to my daughter Eliza. A ridiculously funny, sassy, clever and wise person who I have the pleasure of living with. A powerhouse that the world needs.

My son Cormac is a natural encourager, who smiles, listens and makes you be your best, just to keep up with him. If someone like him believes in you, you feel you can do anything.

Then there's Louise, who's still with me after highs, lows and six lockdowns. Intriguing, engaging, brilliant, and to borrow from Cole Porter, delovely.

